THE COUNTRY INN MYSTERY

An absolutely gripping cozy mystery
for all crime thriller fans

FAITH MARTIN

Travelling Cook Mysteries Book 7

JOFFE
BOOKS

Revised edition 2024
Joffe Books, London
www.joffebooks.com

First published in Great Britain in 2019

This paperback edition was first published
in Great Britain in 2024

Cover art by Nick Castle

ISBN: 978-1-83526-401-0

*For everyone who likes to take a weekend
break — without the murder, of course!*

CHAPTER ONE

Jenny Starling watched the infused milk begin to move gently in the pan, and slipped in the salmon, haddock and hake pieces to poach. She gently prodded a crushed bay leaf down so that its oils would flavour what would then become the sauce for her rich and decadent fish pie, and sighed with satisfaction at the resulting aroma.

Outside, the second week of September had begun gratifyingly warm, and as she glanced out of the Spindlewood Inn's kitchen window, her view of the gardens was bathed in gentle sunlight. Currently looking resplendent with chrysanthemums and other seasonal favourites, they had scattered around the flat lawn a number of wooden picnic tables for al fresco dining.

As this provided an added attraction for guests, the inn's owners, Richard and Muriel Sparkey, were careful to keep the gardens looking their best.

As she set about peeling some luscious prawns to give her pie added 'oomph,' the travelling cook sighed with a sense of genuine pleasure and well-being.

It had been a lucky break for her when her old friend Patsy Vine had recommended her services as stand-in chef here, whilst Patsy took her own annual two-week summer holiday to Italy. Especially since the Spindlewood Inn was situated in the heart of the picturesque Cotswold village of Caulcott Deeping, thus offering a very pleasant working environment to any itinerant chef.

With a tributary of the Windrush river running close by, spanned by any number of pretty arched bridges, it was not surprising that the village had become something of a tourist attraction. Which meant that during the peak summer months there was no shortage of happy Americans, Japanese, Chinese or other European visitors staying in the inn's modest six bedrooms.

But with the advent of September, the rush slowed to a trickle, hence Patsy's late timing of her own summer break. Even so, the Spindlewood Inn was fully booked for that upcoming weekend, thanks to the 'Regency Extravaganza' that was being held there, the brainchild, apparently, of the local historical society and an am-dram group, the Caulcott Deeping Players. With Richard and Muriel's eager consent, naturally, since it meant extra and unexpected revenue for them!

Jenny smiled now as she checked that her beetroot soup starter, (which would be served cold, naturally, with a dollop of basil pesto and some garlic-coated croutons,) was chilling properly in the fridge, and then set about preparing her blackberry and apple roulade.

Naturally, she'd assured her friend that the much-vaunted Regency menu would present no problems for her, and had had to all but chivvy her out of the door when the time came for her to catch her train for the airport. But the moment her friend was safely on her way to Italy, she'd quickly opened up her laptop and done some quick research on Regency dishes. Although she was sure she could cook *anything* required of her, she was not a food historian, nor did she have much knowledge of what they were eating back when Jane Austen was penning her novels!

The themed weekend began this evening — Friday — with the arrival of guests for dinner, and ended with Monday's breakfast. Of course, there were also guests not staying at the inn who had reserved tables — mostly, Jenny surmised, members of the historical society, who would be getting into the spirit by dressing up in Regency-style costumes.

But after an hour or so of frantic googling, any lingering doubts that she might not be able to produce an authentic feast circa 1811–1820 had been laid to rest, and Jenny was now confident that she'd come up with a menu that would please her new employers.

And as if thinking about them had conjured one of them up, she suddenly heard a rustle behind her, and Muriel came quickly through the doorway. It was just gone four o'clock, and although the inn had opened at three-thirty, the locals at least were only interested in alcoholic consumption for the moment.

The guests for the Regency Extravaganza, however, were due to arrive any time between four and six, with their evening dinner due to start at seven-thirty. Luckily, however, before Patsy had left the two cooks had between them managed to do the bulk of the work necessary. And tomorrow Jenny would have the help of two local village women that Muriel had hired — somewhat reluctantly and on an ad hoc basis — to help out when really necessary.

It was from her old friend that Jenny had got the impression that the Sparkeys were very keen to make money, but very reluctant to spend it. Which had prompted Jenny to make sure she got her two weeks' wages paid up front!

Muriel, who had celebrated her fortieth birthday back in April, was around five feet nine inches tall, and with her abundant short curly brown hair, clear complexion and large blue eyes, Jenny supposed she could get away with shaving five years off her age. The cook had also noticed that the landlady tended to speak with a certain amount of care and attention, which led her to suspect that Muriel was suppressing some kind of a strong accent. Cockney maybe?

'Ah, how's it coming Jenny?' she asked now, her eyes darting around the kitchen, taking everything in. She looked relieved to see it neat and tidy but obviously in full production. Then she sniffed appreciatively. 'Something smells good.'

'Probably the poaching fish,' Jenny smiled back.

There was beetroot soup or duck liver pâté with an orange and rocket salad for starters. Then a 'luxury' fish pie, a vegetarian aubergine dish, or a venison casserole for mains, followed by a choice of the roulade or raspberry mousse with shortbread for dessert. All of which was to be rounded off with the usual cheese and biscuit platter.

Muriel watched for a few minutes as Jenny competently set about making the shortbread, adding a touch of lavender to give the dessert a flowery lift. 'Need any help?' she eventually offered.

Jenny glanced up at her, and smiled amiably. 'Only if you're bored and want something to do,' she said lightly. Having got the job on Patsy's say-so rather than on her own merits, she was keen to reassure the landlady that she had everything under control.

Muriel gave a slight shrug. 'I've got half an hour or so. Right now there's only Old Walter out there,' she nodded through the door, where what had once been the living quarters of the old residence now housed the bar, 'and a few anglers telling tall tales about the one that got away. So I'm not exactly expecting a rush.'

'Old Walter?' Jenny echoed. 'He sounds like he might be a bit of a character.'

Muriel rolled her eyes expressively. 'He's a pest is what he is. Ninety if he's a day, he's on the doorstep at the start of every opening hour, smelling faintly of manure and dressed like Worzel Gummidge. He then sits at the bar and orders pint after pint, until he starts to slide off the stool, at which point he staggers home.'

Jenny laughed. 'I hope he manages to get home all right?'

'Oh he does, don't worry. He lives with his long-suffering daughter in one of the farms on the outskirts of the village. I reckon he's got a guardian angel whose sole job it is to make sure that he doesn't wander under the wheels of any passing traffic, or reel off and fall into the brook.'

The brook, Jenny came to realise, was what the locals called the stream that ran so picturesquely through the village, where it eventually formed a large, reed-fringed village pond. Then it meandered off through the water meadows that surrounded the village, to reunite with the Windrush itself just outside a neighbouring town.

'Still, I suppose he provides a bit of local colour,' Muriel conceded reluctantly. 'The tourists love him anyway, so he more than earns his keep,' she admitted pragmatically. 'So, what can I do to help out?'

'How do you feel about peeling carrots and potatoes?' Jenny asked with a grin.

Muriel blinked, then grinned back. 'Well, I asked for it!' she said ruefully.

Jenny watched as she reached for a potato peeler, and as Muriel pulled up the sleeves of her sweater to avoid them getting wet, she saw the beginnings of a tattoo on her left arm. All Jenny could make out was a pair of talons — obviously from some fabulous bird of prey — that held a coloured ribbon or banner of some sort.

And once again, Jenny was convinced that Muriel had not grown up in the rarefied and genteel surroundings of the Cotswolds. Perhaps she was from somewhere up north, and the tattoo revealed allegiance to some football club or other? Evidence of a more rough-and-ready past that she was trying to leave behind her, perhaps?

And if that was true, more power to her, Jenny thought with a subtle nod of approval as she set about grinding some peppercorns to add to the water biscuits for the cheese platter.

People grew up and moved on, and what was wrong with that?

* * *

Half an hour later, the first of their weekend guests arrived: a middle-aged American couple, whose presence was clearly announced by a pair of loud, friendly voices that reached back even to the furthest recesses of the kitchen.

With a muttered, 'Oh heck, here we go,' Muriel abandoned Jenny to the root vegetables and shot through the door, where the cook heard her greeting them warmly.

'Mr and Mrs Buckey, how are you? I'm so glad you could make it, and welcome to the Spindlewood Inn. I hope you had a good journey?'

Curious, Jenny moved to the door of the kitchen and glanced across the narrow corridor and into the open doorway beyond, where she could see a portion of the public bar.

'Thank you, ma'am, we did. I'm Silas and this is my wife, Min.' The man who was talking was in his mid-fifties and heavyset. Balding, with tufts of white hair over both his ears which matched his thick white eyebrows, he had a ferocious tan, and looked as if he should be wearing a Stetson. Rarely had Jenny seen someone who matched a stereotype so perfectly.

At barely five feet two, his wife had stylish blonde hair and hazel eyes. She was dressed in an eye-catching kaftan in various tones of aqua and blue, and had a large white bag over her shoulder that looked as if it should cost a sum that was well into three figures. Layers of beads and bangles tinkled musically whenever she moved.

'We've come from London, so it took us only a couple hours on the train,' this vision now confessed with a happy laugh. 'I just love how everything is in such easy reach of everything else over here,' she gushed, sounding even more American than her husband. 'We're going on to see Stratford-upon-Avon next week — I just adore Shakespeare — and that'll take us hardly any time at all either! In the States, it takes ages to get anywhere — unless you fly all the time.'

Jenny, buoyed up by this display of such uncomplicated good cheer, turned back to cutting out her shortbread dough into pretty star-shaped designs with one of her favourite stainless-steel cutters.

'Everything's so exciting! We can't wait to wear our costumes, can we, Si?' Min Buckey's voice rang out happily.

'We've rented them for the weekend from this really great little place we found in Soho. Haven't we, Si?'

'Yes, sweetie.'

'The man there assured me that they were made from authentic designs that were being worn when Jane Austen was living in Bath. Oh, we're going to see Bath before going on to Stratford, aren't we, Si?'

'We sure are, sweetie.'

'Do we wear them tonight? Our costumes, I mean?'

Jenny grinned, listening as Muriel told her that the dinner tonight did indeed start off with the first of the 'scenes' to be given by the am-dram players, and that of course, the Buckeys were welcome to wear their costumes if they wanted to.

'Several members of the local historical society are also participating in the weekend, and are bound to be in costume too,' Muriel informed them.

'That's great. I can't wait for the plays to begin. I just adore a good love story, don't I, Si? That's why, when I saw this advertised, I said to Si, we've just got to go. To think, we get to be part of a real live tragedy!'

In the kitchen Jenny blinked, not quite sure what to make of that. Usually tragedy didn't instil such gushing enthusiasm. Curious now, Jenny set the biscuits to bake in the oven and then picked up the booklet that Patsy had given her. Pulling up a kitchen chair, she sat down and began to read the brochure.

The Regency Extravaganza, it seemed, was intent on 'celebrating' and 'recreating' the 'famous but tragic love story' of the village's local gentry.

According to 'legend based on true facts,' in the early 1800s the local lord of the manor, one Sir Hugh Rowland (whose family still lived in the impressive 1750s Caulcott House to this day), was married to the beautiful, much younger, Lady Hester Mainwaring. Hester's father and Sir Hugh had arranged this match, which was to their mutual advantage, and involved the exchange of land and monies on

Sir Mainwaring's part, and some patents on the part of Sir Hugh. No doubt the match had been financially beneficial to all concerned, although it quickly became clear that the young and spirited Hester hadn't taken kindly to being married off to a man her father's age. And one, moreover, with something of a reputation as a roué and gambler. Many a hapless village maid, it seemed, had had youngsters tugging at their skirts who bore a marked resemblance to the lord of the manor.

From the start, so local gossip had it, the marriage was rocky and ill-fated, with things finally coming to a head when the lovely Lady Hester met and fell in love with the younger son of another local landowner, one Mr Reginald Truby. As a younger son, Reginald wasn't even due to inherit his father's land, and like most of his kind, was fated to make a choice of either the army or the clergy for a career. So although he was both dashing and handsome (naturally, Jenny mused cynically!) he would hardly have measured up as husband material for the regal Lady Hester, even if she hadn't been so inconveniently already married.

Of course, the young lovers were discovered one dark and fateful day, and Sir Hugh, as the wronged and cuckolded husband, duly challenged the young dandy Reginald to a duel at dawn the following day.

Again Jenny paused in her perusal of this somewhat dubious account, and sighed heavily. Why did duels always have to be fought at dawn? And weren't they made illegal at some point in history? (Jenny noted, with a smile, that in the weekend schedule, and for the purposes of the participants who would be witnessing this exciting re-enactment, 'dawn' had been shifted to a far more convenient ten o'clock in the morning.)

Not at all convinced of how true these 'true facts' were, Jenny nevertheless carried on reading, fascinated in spite of her amused scepticism.

According to local legend, Sir Hugh, as well as being a shocking ladies' man and an unrepentant gambler, was also clearly a coward (or else he held firm and understandable ideas on the necessity of preserving his own skin, depending on your point of view). For, in a 'dastardly act of wanton wickedness' he arranged with his second, a similarly venal character by the name of Sir Francis Gordon, to tamper with Truby's pistol before the start of the duel, thus rendering it useless.

Naturally, Sir Hugh survived the duel. Equally naturally, Truby did not.

However, Truby's own second (presumably someone possessed of a less venal character, Jenny surmised with a snort) and a number of other impartial witnesses smelled a rat, and demanded to inspect both sets of pistols. After which Sir Hugh, no doubt very sensibly deciding that discretion was the better part of valour, promptly hopped back onto his horse and galloped off. And presumably at a fair old rate of knots, since although the rest of the outraged party chased him as far as Bristol, they singularly failed to catch up with him. Historians believed that he then boarded the first boat he could find. It was thereafter rumoured that he spent the rest of his nefarious days in (luxurious) disgrace somewhere near where Juan-les-Pins is situated nowadays.

Gracious, Jenny thought, as she turned the final lurid page. They didn't half know how to go about things in days of yore!

Reading on determinedly to the end, it transpired, however, that things didn't go so well for Lady Hester. Left inconsolable at the loss of her one true love, she promptly drowned herself, thus becoming immortalised forever.

Jenny sighed as she folded the brochure in half and dropped it into the bin under the sink. But she could see that it certainly made a good tale for guests, and would be sure to please the effervescent Min's taste for gothic romance.

According to the itinerary, the Extravaganza also included a visit to Caulcott House and gardens, to see where the tragic Hester and the infamous Sir Hugh had once lived. And peppered throughout the three days, the am-dram players were going to regale the guests with scenes from their story, which included the famous duel (to take place in a nearby farmer's field) and the suicide of the tragic heroine in the village pond. Which, Jenny noted with a grin, had now been relabelled — far more romantically — as a 'lake.' Which was understandable, she allowed magnanimously. After all, drowning yourself in the duck pond just didn't have the same cachet, did it?

Jenny noticed that a visit to a local 'eyecatcher' (whatever that was) and a night-time 'ghost walk' (which was already an established entertainment during the tourist season) were also available on request.

And Jenny wished them the best of British luck!

* * *

At five o'clock, and with everything ticking over nicely in the kitchen, Jenny made her way to the top floor and down a narrow corridor to her rooms under the eaves, where she'd dumped her luggage. To her right was a small living space, with a large sofa set against the internal wall facing a skylight, which had been installed when the house had been converted into an inn. This window, as well as letting in much needed light, also gave her a view across the undeniably pretty village square, with a view of a Jubilee oak and the grey square tur- reted tower of a Norman church. This room also packed in a small kitchenette area where Jenny could at least make herself a late-night cup of cocoa without having to go downstairs to the kitchen.

Further down the narrow corridor, a door to the right opened out onto a bathroom — which wasn't big enough to have an actual bath in it, but did at least hold a shower tall enough for Jenny to stand up in.

But it was the bedroom just opposite that was clearly going to give her the most trouble, she realised glumly as she stood in the doorway looking around. Here the roof sloped up into a deep inverted 'V' either side of the central space, leaving only the very middle of the room with an apex high enough for her to walk through without bumping her head. The bed, a rather frugal single, was placed against one wall. She tentatively stretched herself out full length on it, relieved to find that her feet didn't actually hang over the bottom end of the mattress. And it was as she was contemplating the sloped ceiling that seemed to be hovering not far above her nose that she clearly heard, through the thin partition wall behind her, a voice.

A very angry voice.

'Bloody hell, Vince, this is the absolute limit! How am I supposed to dress and do my make-up in *here*? There isn't even room to swing the proverbial cat! I should have demanded one of the guest rooms. Bloody Matt, I'm going to literally kill the little sod when I see him! You know he was the one who put us up for this pitiful little gig? Didn't I say it was too insignificant for us to bother with? And the fee is peanuts. But no, everyone else wanted to do it because it would be good practice for you all, and I let myself be persuaded. It would be fun, you said. Fun? Huh!'

Jenny, on the bed, closed her eyes and counted slowly to ten.

Clearly the 'spare' junk room at the very end of the attic had been allocated as a dressing room for the Caulcott Deeping Amateur Dramatic Society. And, just as clearly, she would have no peace whilst they were using it.

With a sigh, Jenny swung her legs over the bed, sat up and promptly bumped her head on the ceiling. She swore roundly, using a good mixture of Anglo-Saxon rhetoric, but was careful to do so under her breath. Then, with tight-lipped patience, she set about unpacking her suitcases, and stowed them away carefully under the bed.

As she stepped out into the corridor however, the woman's voice in the end room once again piped up.

'Pass me my make-up bag, would you, Vince? I've just bought that Rory Gee toner and I want to try it out. It's ruinously expensive, of course, but so worth it, even for this penny-ante little show. It's so much better for the skin than . . .'

Jenny, not wishing to hear anything more from the prima donna in the other room, beat a hasty retreat back to her kitchen.

Venison casserole had more class than to throw hissy fits.

CHAPTER TWO

'Ricky, Malc's just phoned,' Muriel's voice called in from the bar and carried through into the kitchen with ease. 'He can't do the ghost walk tonight, but I told him not to worry. With the first big scene from the am-dram people due at nine, he probably wouldn't get any contenders anyway! He says he'll come on Sunday night instead.'

In the kitchen, Jenny smiled across the table at Richard Sparkey. Somewhere in his mid-forties, the landlord of the Spindlewood Inn was a few inches shorter than Jenny, with thinning sandy hair and wide hazel eyes. A smattering of freckles across his nose and cheeks made him look a bit like an overgrown schoolboy. He had just enough of a paunch to make him look cuddly, but still dressed well. With a rather big mouth that looked slightly goofy but appealing whenever he smiled — which was often — he looked every inch the picture of a welcoming landlord.

He'd come into the kitchen a few minutes ago to make himself a large sandwich, cheerfully stating that Jenny didn't need to interrupt her preparations to see to his needs. Now he walked to the open door and called through the corridor to his wife. 'Fine, but tell him the American couple definitely want to do something Sunday night, so he can't back out. Min's determined to see a spook of some kind before going back to the States, or so she says. And she's managed to persuade quite a crowd from the historical society that it'll be interesting as well.'

'OK.'

He wandered back into the kitchen, eyeing their temporary cook thoughtfully as he continued to chew hungrily on his mammoth BLT. She was certainly big and beautiful and knew her stuff. 'We like to encourage Malcolm and his spook-hunters whenever we can because after searching for spirits in the churchyard, they tend to come back here and buy spirits at the bar.' He grinned at his own joke. 'We lay in a special brandy and cognac that we swear helps steady the nerves in case of ghosts,' he added shamelessly.

And naturally, Jenny mused, the cognac or brandy would be age-old and very expensive — and probably bought on an away-day booze cruise to Calais! Patsy was right: as well as pinching the pennies, her employers chased them with unremitting ferocity. Mind you, it was almost impossible to take offence with the ever-affable Richard.

'Looks like our most distinguished guest has just arrived,' Richard said suddenly, quickly swallowing the last mouthful of sandwich with an audible gulp and washing it down with a sip from his half-pint glass of cider shandy.

And from the direction of the bar Jenny could, indeed, clearly hear a well-educated masculine voice giving a low bass rumble of greeting to the landlady.

She raised one eyebrow in query towards the landlord.

'Dr Rory Gilchrist — our don from Oxford,' he supplied obligingly. 'He tutors in modern history at St Bede's College, so I suppose I can see why this Regency weekend thing might appeal to him. But I'd have thought it would have too much populist appeal to attract the likes of him. Unless he has a penchant for amateur dramatics himself,' he added, his eyes gleaming in speculation. 'You never know with that lot,' he added, mock darkly.

'It takes all sorts,' Jenny agreed. 'Perhaps he just likes to watch pretty actresses in high-waistline dresses?'

'Don't we all?' Richard sighed elaborately. 'But seriously, I don't quite understand why he's bothered to book the room for all three nights. Oxford isn't that far away is it? He could drive it easily.'

Jenny shrugged. 'Perhaps he just wants a break from all those dreaming spires? All that academia must get tiring sometimes.'

Richard shrugged, obviously losing interest but listening absently as his wife soft-soaped their newest guest into signing the register and then making pointed noises about his suitcases. This none-too-subtle call to arms had Richard abandoning his drink with a sigh and going out to offer to take them upstairs.

Jenny, curious in spite of herself, moved to the door and glanced across the narrow corridor and through into the bar. There she saw a tall man just as he turned away from the bar and glanced through to the dining area, which was situated at the far end of the room. His face, in profile, did indeed look suitably patrician, with a clean-shaven chin and thin aesthetic nose, as befitted an erudite man of learning. His neatly cut hair was the very attractive colour of old gold just turning to silver, and when he turned back to thank Richard for taking his cases, Jenny could just see that his eyes were a very pale colour — maybe blue, grey or green.

Mostly definitely Patsy would have called him a silver fox! And definitely too good-looking to be single, Jenny rather thought. Ah well, she mused philosophically. Perhaps it was just as well that she was only here to cook!

And speaking of which, she returned without any real regret to her kitchen and began to grate a mixture of local cheeses to top her fish pie.

* * *

The dining room of the Spindlewood Inn led off from the main bar room through an open interior arch. And although it wasn't Jenny's place as the cook to check it (that was

15

the responsibility of Muriel or the waitresses, two younger women hired from the village to help out in busy times), she always liked to see for herself where her food would be served. Just to satisfy herself that it would do her cooking justice.

So just before seven-thirty, she found herself standing in the middle of the room and looking around her with a sense of genuine pleasure. In keeping with the age of the inn, floorboards had been left exposed and had darkened with age to a shade of near black. Large, dark oak tables and matching chairs littered the space, lending the small and cosy room an ambience of comfortable solidity. This was enhanced by an ancient and venerable red flock wallpaper that had long since mellowed to a respectable rose colour, and a grandmother clock, standing against one now disused chimney breast, ticked away ponderously but pleasingly. At two tall sash windows long velvet curtains in dark cream were tied back with old-fashioned fringed bell ropes, giving a lovely elegant touch to the room and hinting at past decadence.

The tables themselves were covered with simple cream linen tablecloths and napkins, with maroon place mats and silver cruet sets, and in the centre, each table had a simple small cream vase full of mixed flowers picked straight from the gardens.

Jenny nodded. Yes — it would set off her food well.

She stepped through the archway and headed back past the bar. A young man was just approaching it from the opposite side, and when he spoke his voice, which most definitely had the tell-tale song of Wales in it, had her turning her head in instant admiration.

'Hello there. Ion Dryfuss. I'm here for the Regency weekend? I have a single room booked, I think.'

The voice rose and fell with such a lilt that he sounded as if he was singing rather than merely talking, and Jenny, who had always loved the broad Welsh accent, found her steps slowing so that she might hear more of it.

Muriel beamed her usual fulsome welcome at the young stranger. Somewhere in his late twenties or maybe just about early thirties, Jenny judged, he was her own height, and dressed in much-washed, tight-fitting jeans and a plain white shirt. He had the elegant and lean body of a dancer, giving an impression of wiry strength beneath all that boneless fluidity.

'Oh yes, Mr Dryfuss. Room 4. I do hope you'll like it. It has a lovely view over the gardens.' As Muriel reached behind her for his key, the young man turned, looking around and giving Jenny a glimpse of his triangular face. It had a strong pointed chin and cheekbones so sharp that she could have carved a nice slice of Parma ham on them. His hair was brown and curly, his eyes a matching deep, dark brown. And right now they were widening on her and taking her in with a slightly startled expression.

But Jenny was used to this — at nearly six feet in height, with extreme curves in all the right places, bountiful near-black hair and blue eyes that many men had described as 'spectacular,' she'd always enjoyed her fair share of masculine attention. Although hardly the slim, fair-haired vision of what most modern-day men assumed was their female idyll, the travelling cook had her own undeniable style. So far, though, Jenny had yet to find herself what her old granny would have called a proper 'keeper.'

But in this particular case, whether or not the young Welshman could properly be listed amongst those who found her attractive was hard to say, as his expression gave little away. His slight smile suggested that he certainly appreciated her presence, but there was a distinct lack of interest in his gaze that made her wonder.

Gay or not gay, Jenny mused idly.

'Is that all your luggage Mr Dryfuss?' Muriel asked now, indicating the single dark green carrying case that was sitting at his feet.

'Yes, I have a large satchel in my car with all my art supplies, but that can stay in the boot. And I haven't bought a costume, I'm afraid. I forgot all about that aspect of it, idiot that I am, and then couldn't find a costume shop at the last minute that had anything I liked the look of.'

'Oh I'm sure that doesn't matter,' Muriel assured him with a bright smile. 'It's strictly optional. I'm sure you won't be the only one in civvies!'

'That's a relief. I don't want to be thought of as a spoilsport.'

Again, Jenny felt as if she could listen to him speak all day long. With that lovely Welsh-valleys sing-song accent, he could recite a list of plumbing supplies and make it sound divine.

'So you're an artist?' Muriel made conversation pleasantly.

'Hardly! But I do have a rather shameful hobby that I wouldn't like to admit to in public,' the young man teased her, leaning one bony elbow on the bar.

Playing along, Muriel leaned across and lowered her voice. 'Go on. You can tell me. I won't tell a soul.' And so saying, she did a cross-your-heart gesture with her right hand.

Up the bar a ways, an old man, who from the way he was dressed could only be Old Walter, leaned sideways a bit, his ancient ears clearly flapping.

'All right. But make sure you keep it under your hat mind,' Ion Dryfuss warned, lowering his voice dramatically. 'Especially from your vicar. Men of the cloth especially don't like the kinds of things I get up to.'

'Oooh, now you've got me really worried,' Muriel gushed. 'What exactly do you do? Paint naked vicars?'

'Worse!' Ian leaned even closer and stage-whispered, 'Brass rubbing.' He moved back, wide-eyed and nodding emphatically.

Muriel burst out laughing.

Old Walter sighed, and took a disappointed sup from his pint of beer.

Jenny, unashamedly eavesdropping and grinning as well, reluctantly decided that she needed to get back to the kitchen for the final rush of preparation.

'Well, I never heard the like,' Muriel continued to josh, as Jenny scooted past the side entrance to the bar and across the corridor into her kitchen. 'You might just have time for a quick drink before dinner if you hurry,' she heard the land-lady encourage him. 'Hope you enjoy your stay.'

'Oh I'm sure I will,' the young Welshman predicted cheerfully.

* * *

In the kitchen, Jenny opened all the windows to allow the warm September breeze to dissipate some of the steam and heat. The waitresses had arrived an hour before, two women so alike that they could have been sisters, and had introduced themselves as Mags and Babs.

Now Jenny set about overseeing the final hectic ten minutes or so before dinner was served. She was so busy making sure that everything was just right that she only gradually became aware that she was hearing voices coming in through the kitchen windows from the gardens outside.

She was adding aubergines to a red-hot griddle in order to complete the vegetarian option when she first noticed them; and only then because of the dramatic quality of the voices.

'*You vile strumpet! I rue the day you* . . . What the hell is it? Ruined the family name?' The voice was male, and rather apologetic.

'How the hell should I know?' The female voice that answered was definitely the same as the one Jenny had heard complaining about the size of the dressing room earlier. 'I've got enough to do remembering my own lines, Vince! Look at the script, for Pete's sake. No! Hold on a sec, I just want to record this on my tablet so I can check back on it later and make sure . . . OK. Got it. Now . . . *How dare you, husband, traduce me when your own perverse humours and unnatural practices have so corrupted our most unhappy union.*'

Jenny found herself ensnared by the voice. But this time it was not by a regional singsong accent, but by the sensual, husky and throbbing tonal quality of the female vocal chords.

For whoever the petulant actress was, when she put her mind to it, her voice was unmistakably impressive. Smoky, with a deep but unforced timbre to it that you could almost feel reverberating in your chest cavity.

'*I have corrupted it? When it is you who has taken a lover?*' the unseen Vince shot back.

And Jenny was so looking forward to hearing the actress's reply that she almost forgot to turn her aubergines over, so that both sides would show that beautiful grilled horizontal lines of scorched flesh that you only got when grilled properly.

'*Oh, do not speak Reginald's name!* Wait, let me play that bit back . . .'

Jenny sighed, and forcing her focus away from the rehearsing actors, rescued her aubergines and moved from the window to take the trays of mousse from the fridge. Mousse, in her opinion, shouldn't be served totally cold and frigid straight from the fridge, since the flavours of fruit were never at their best when utterly chilled. They needed to be introduced to room temperature to bring out the tang of their flavours.

From outside, she heard the playback of the actress's recorded voice repeating her lines. And Jenny had to admit that though she might be a bit of a prima donna, she certainly knew how to pack her lines with punch. And if her physical performance matched that of her vocal talents then the guests of the Regency Extravaganza were probably going to be in for a real treat.

'Vince, you *are* sure that Philip notified the local press about this weekend, aren't you?' the woman went on to demand. 'I mean, with a proper photographer and everything? Only I've got an audition for another ad next Wednesday in Cheltenham, and if I can get my photo in the papers at the same time, it might just impress . . .'

With a sigh, Jenny firmly closed the window.

* * *

Dinner was a triumph — naturally. Muriel, looking very pleased, relayed several 'compliments to the chef' throughout the hour and a half that she, Mags and Babs were serving, and by the end of it, Jenny was feeling sufficiently appreciated for her efforts.

Free now to hover in the archway to the dining room and watch for herself the first of the am-dram scenes, she was keen to put faces to the voices — especially that of the smoky-voiced, whining prima donna. Like most people, Jenny felt the attraction of a bit of live theatre.

All the tables were full of replete and happy diners, she noticed with satisfaction, with Min and Silas Buckey looking particularly resplendent in their costumes. Several of the other ladies had their hair dressed up and bedecked with fake jewels, or were wearing wigs that had been set in ornate ringlets, and many of the gentlemen wore silver-and-gold embroidered silk outfits.

Other guests — including both the Oxford don and the foxy-faced lad from the Welsh valleys — were wearing nothing more remarkable than trousers, shirt and jacket; plain dark blue in the case of Dr Gilchrist, and grey in the case of Ion Dryfuss.

This mixed message gave the dining room an odd, somewhat surreal feel, but with the dramatic entrance of the two leading actors, who swept past Jenny without a second glance, it hardly mattered, as all attention immediately settled on 'Sir Hugh' and 'Lady Hester.'

Jenny's first glimpse of the sultry-voiced prima donna wasn't a disappointment, and she could see the guests at the tables all felt the same way.

Nearly Jenny's own height, but considerably more svelte of figure, she had long dark brown hair that had been swept up in a very fetching Regency hairstyle. This had the effect of showing off not only her milky swan-like neck to its full advantage, but also cleverly framed the full beauty of her face. And it was definitely some face, Jenny acknowledged without a modicum of envy. Long, oval, pale, and with high cheekbones, it reminded the travelling cook of the faces she'd seen painted by some of the more famous pre-Raphaelite artists.

Her costume was made of pale green sprigged muslin, with the high waistline that viewers of BBC Jane Austen costume dramas would easily recognise, and flowed in straight, neat folds to fall on the top of some silk slippers in a matching hue. On her arm hung a rather large black velvet and lace-trimmed reticule, embroidered with pretty beading and pulled together with a drawstring clasp.

More than one or two members of the local historical society nodded approval at the accuracy of her gown, and Jenny wondered how the actress had managed to come by it. It had clearly been made for her by someone very clever with a needle, and looked exquisite — and expensive. It was obviously not a rental from a costume shop.

Jenny, standing in the shadows to one side in the arch, watched the little drama with a mixture of amusement and interest. Big, bad Sir Hugh, it seemed, had been taunted by some of the 'young bucks' at his gentleman's gaming club, implying that he was being cuckolded by the young son of a local upstart and insignificant landowner.

Lady Hester demurely denied it, naturally, and put in a few hints of her own that her husband's gaming was getting out of hand.

As the two protagonists, with flowery phrases and much sweeping about between the tables (presumably in order to engage all their audience in the drama and make them feel they as if they were getting their money's worth), continued to spar, Jenny's attention began to drift towards the diners themselves.

Many of the locals and historical society members were obviously wrapped up in the story and performance being given. But Jenny noticed, with a hint of surprise, that Dr Rory Gilchrist was almost alone in the company, in that he seemed to be watching Sir Hugh's performance more closely than that of Lady Hester. Whilst, interestingly enough, the handsome young Welshman's eyes seemed to be fixed on the actress, whose husky, sexy voice so effortlessly filled the room. But was he merely admiring her elegant appearance and theatrical performance, as gay men sometimes did (if he was in fact gay), or was it the actress herself who was captivating him? In which case, he was very much heterosexual!

As Sir Hugh and Lady Hester's quarrel rose to ever more acrimonious heights, culminating with Sir Hugh finally warning his wife that if he found her in young Truby's company again that 'dire consequences would ensue to that villain's detriment,' Jenny's attention wandered on to the American couple.

Min, dressed in something that looked more Victorian than Regency, and bedecked with diamonds that Jenny sincerely hoped were paste, was clearly enjoying herself enormously, and following the theatrics with avid, shining eyes. Her husband too looked amused and entertained, and there was no question that he had eyes only for the young actress.

A sudden wave of applause alerted Jenny to the fact that the performance was over, and the next instant a furious-faced Sir Hugh stormed past her, followed more demurely by his wife. After a few seconds the two of them returned to the dining room and took a bow, then disappeared again, presumably to change into their normal clothes.

Jenny, with a gentle sigh, made her way back to the kitchen, where she made sure that Mags and Babs had left everything in good order for the following morning.

* * *

When Jenny made her way through to the bar about an hour later, it was clear that the actors were still in residence, back in their civvies and holding court at opposite ends of the room. The coterie around the actress, naturally, was far larger than that of the one around Vince/Sir Hugh.

Jenny, ordering a large gin and tonic from Richard behind the bar (one drink per night was part of her wages!), made her way casually over towards the less crowded end of the room and took a window seat at a small table for two.

Perhaps she should put kedgeree back on the breakfast menu? Her thoughts of old-fashioned culinary delights were interrupted when she noticed the last few members of the historical society take their leave of Vince, stranding him with only a glass of wine for company.

Without his costume and wig he was revealed as a sixty-something man with white hair and rather weak-looking brown eyes. He smiled affably as Dr Rory Gilchrist approached him. Clearly, Jenny mused, the two men must already know each other.

'Rory — so what did you think?' he asked, confirming her guess. 'Not bad for an old ham, eh?' He was clearly feeling flushed with success over his performance.

'Does the Law Society know what their supposedly respectable rural solicitors get up to in their spare time?' Rory asked archly. 'And those silk trousers of yours looked painfully tight.'

'Oh don't remind me — they pinched like crazy. Still, at least I didn't have to fake having a face like a sour lemon. Did it show from the way I walked?'

The Oxford don laughed genially. 'No, you were all right.'

'And now I suppose you want an introduction to the lovely Rachel Norman?' Vince asked dryly, nodding across the room to where his fellow actor was now holding court. 'Most men do!'

'She's quite something,' Rory agreed carelessly, following his line of sight. 'And that voice! What a pity she can't actually act.'

Vince gave a surprised bark of laughter and discreetly turned it into a cough. Over her gin and tonic Jenny bit back her own desire to laugh. So she'd not been the only one to notice a certain stiffness and overdone theatricality about the woman's performance.

'Don't tell her that for Pete's sake,' Vince pleaded. 'She'll go right for your jugular! As it is she's the leading light of our little am-dram group, and the only one of us with any professional credits to her name.'

Rory's eyes widened. 'You're joking! You mean she's actually been on a professional stage? Doing what — walk-on parts?'

'Don't be unkind,' Vince said, but without any real heat. Clearly the prima donna considered herself to be a cut above her fellow am-dram members, and in Jenny's experience people with such a high opinion of themselves weren't usually all that good at making friends with others.

'As a matter of fact it wasn't the stage — it was television,' Vince continued, correcting his friend with a wry smile. 'Oh, not an actual programme, just some adverts.'

'Ah,' Rory said. 'But I don't recall seeing that face on the screen, even trying to sell me something.'

Vince laughed. 'Shussh, she'll hear you! Actually, her first break was as a hand model for a designer hand lotion. She has such lovely long fingers and slender hands, if you care to notice. And just recently she did a voice-over for those lingerie ads. You know the ones . . .'

He went on to describe a recent advert for some saucy underwear that, now that it had been mentioned, rang a distant bell for Jenny too. She'd thought that sexy voice had sounded vaguely familiar!

'And of course, with a voice like hers, she's just signed a contract to do some more. She's all set to go to the studios soon to do the recordings.'

'Good for her,' Rory said, without much interest.

'Of course, what she really wants is to be a legitimate and very *well-paid* actress, naturally,' Vince added with a knowing smile. 'She sees our poor little group very much as a stop-gap, I'm sorry to say. What's worse, our little gigs barely keep her in pocket money. And who knows — perhaps the ads *will* turn out to be a stepping stone for her. She has a way of wrapping people — and by that I mean men, naturally — around her little finger. So maybe one of the production people will be able to get her an audition for something better.'

'A bit part in a soap opera?' Rory volunteered, again without much interest. 'Vince, I really need to speak to you about that little problem of mine . . .' Here the Oxford don suddenly lowered his voice and looked around. And instantly spotted Jenny, sitting unobtrusively at the nearby table and now looking vacantly out of the window at the darkened village square beyond.

'You know, that little matter I told you about last week? It's becoming more and more urgent. She's already driven me out of Oxford — that's the main reason why I signed up for this little shindig of yours, to give me a bit of respite from her for a few days. Perhaps we can go to my room . . . ?' And so saying, out of the corner of her eye, Jenny noticed the academic take his friend firmly by the elbow and begin steering him away.

Jenny, deciding that it was high time that she too went to bed, tossed back the last of her nightcap and made her way towards the bar. As she did so, she passed by the outer fringes of the crowd grouped around the husky-voiced Rachel.

'Now, Mr Buckey, you're making me very jealous! You really have tickets at Stratford to see David Tennant? What's he playing in — Richard II, is it? Or is it one of the other kings? Whatever, I'm *so* envious.'

Jenny, glancing across the gaggle of heads, was just in time to see the American grin happily. 'Oh, I don't claim to know much about Shakespeare. But when in Rome and all that . . .' Silas shrugged one meaty shoulder in mock modesty.

'And I'd bet a globetrotter such as yourself has actually been to Rome, am I right?' Rachel carried right on flirting.

Even dressed in tight black designer jeans with a plain white silk men's shirt left to drape loosely across her hips, the actress looked good. Real gold glittered at her ears and throat, and as she spoke she reached out and tapped him playfully on the top of his arm.

Silas preened happily.

By his side, his wife looked unhappy at her husband's obvious pleasure at being flirted with by a pretty girl, and sipped morosely at a Bloody Mary.

Jenny was just about to slip past the bar and into the corridor, where the door at the far end gave access to the upper floors, when her glance happened to collide with a familiar and attractive face.

Ion Dryfuss was watching the exchange between Silas Buckey and Rachel intently. And something about the look on his face chilled her to the bone.

Quickly turning away from it, Jenny felt a hand reach out and land gently on her left wrist. She looked down with some surprise at the dirty fingernails and then up into an ancient, wizened face.

'Hello. You're a sight for sore eyes! A gal with a proper figure! Make an old man very happy and have a drink with me?'

Jenny smiled back at Old Walter. No doubt the village eccentric wanted her to buy him his next round. Still, a compliment was a compliment!

With a shrug, she nodded patiently. 'Well, how could a gal refuse an offer like that?' she asked, her blue eyes twinkling.

CHAPTER THREE

'You really shouldn't encourage the old rascal,' Richard Sparkey warned her, but had already poured out a pint and was moving it across the bar towards the old man.

Not surprisingly, Old Walter pounced on it with glee.

He was one of those men who could have been any age between sixty and ninety, and had deeply tanned and weathered skin. His wildly unkempt hair needed trimming and he was wearing a distinctly disreputable pair of faded brown corduroy trousers held up by bright and incongruous scarlet braces. His Hawaiian-style shirt was two sizes too big. Boots so ancient that they could have featured on the *Antiques Roadshow* were hooked carefully around and under the rungs of his barstool, cannily anchoring the old man to his seating.

'Thank you, young lady, you're a gentleman,' he said, somewhat confusingly, as he pulled his pint glass possessively towards him. 'And don't be fooled by what young Richard here has to say. He doesn't in the least object to pulling the pints for me. In fact, the more of 'em the better you like it, eh, Dickie boy? Must fill up the coffers! Just make sure you don't serve 'em to any minors or let one of the trustees catch you swearing, eh?' And so saying, he began to chuckle.

Richard Sparkey shook his head wearily. 'Give it a rest, Walter, or I'll bar you,' he threatened, but his voice sounded more resigned than genuinely aggrieved.

It certainly made Walter chuckle even more. 'Go on, tell her how you and the missus have to be paragons of the community or else,' Walter egged him on.

Seeing Jenny's bemused expression, her employer smiled weakly. 'Old Walter thinks it funny, the unusual way that we came by the inn,' he explained. Resting his elbows on the bar, he lowered his head and voice in the gesture common of a man about to impart a confidence. Obligingly, Jenny also moved a step closer and lowered her head until they were only inches apart.

'Most pub landlords are either employed to run their premises by a brewery, or, if they're running a freehouse, by either buying a building outright and getting all the relevant licences — the lucky buggers — or else getting a business loan and a mortgage from a bank.'

'Right,' Jenny said, following him so far without much difficulty.

But Walter chuffed into his beer at this. 'Go on, tell 'er about old Celia Grimmett. That family always was bonkers! Everyone in the village knows that. Her father was a lay preacher at the chapel. Never would let his womenfolk wear trousers! Hah, wish he would have — old Ma Grimmett had legs like tree trunks.'

Jenny, feeling more bemused than ever, again turned to Richard Sparkey for enlightenment.

Richard sighed. 'This place used to belong to an old lady called Celia Grimmett. It was just a large family home back then — one of many properties that they owned and used to rent out to utterly respectable, middle-class people. Like Old Walter here said, her parents were puritans, and wouldn't have approved of pubs. So, on the face of it, a person less likely to bankroll an inn is hard to imagine.'

'Ah. But I reckon old Celia always did have a bit of a spark left in her, even if she was careful to hide it!' Old Walter put in helpfully here, nodding his head enthusiastically.

'Anyway,' Richard swept on hastily, 'when the village pub went belly up ten years ago, the local mafia — sorry, the parish council and other concerned citizens — approached Celia for help. Saying how much a community needed a local gathering spot and all that, and I dare say it appealed to the old bird's sense of civic duty or something. Anyway, the upshot was she agreed to allow this place,' Richard nodded around him, 'to be converted into a "proper" inn. It had to offer rooms for guests, and serve food provided by local farmers, thus becoming a little more upmarket then a mere pub. She also agreed to let us buy our ales from our local artisan breweries. Although she herself would never set foot in here once we started selling alcohol, mind,' he added with a grin.

This sent Walter off into another paroxysm of childish chuckling.

'And although she agreed a private mortgage arrangement with me and Muriel, there were certain other conditions attached,' Richard admitted. 'As you can imagine, for a woman of strict principles they were rather old-fashioned. In short, it stated that my wife and I had to be "sober and upright" law-abiding citizens, and generally be above reproach in all ways.'

'I'll say. No swearing now, Dickie my boy, or you'll be out on your ear,' Walter crowed.

Jenny blinked. 'Is he serious? Surely she couldn't have imposed conditions on you as Draconian as that!'

Richard smiled and gave a brief shrug. 'Well, yes and no. It's called a "moral turpitude" clause or some such,' Richard laughed. 'It's to do with us being upstanding and honest citizens of Caulcott Deeping, and not bringing shame on the grand Grimmett name.' He rolled his eyes and shook his head. 'Celia's dead now, bless her, but the conditions of the mortgage technically still hold, although the trustees she appointed . . . well, let's just say they don't mind turning a bit of a blind eye to any violations of the more minor kind. Like staying open on a Sunday every now and then.'

'More honoured in the . . . whatnot . . . than in actuality,' Jenny offered, rather lackadaisically.

Richard nodded. 'Exactly. And it's not much of a problem, to be honest. If we swear or use bad language, or if we get drunk ourselves, or behave badly in public, then the mortgage could, technically, be revoked.' Richard shrugged. 'Luckily, neither Muriel nor me drink much — which is just as well. The payments are enormous! But once the last one's finally paid, this place,' Richard nodded around him to indicate the inn, 'will be all ours, free and clear, which has always been our dream,' he finished, with a note of pride.

'And then you can swear at me as much as you like, young Dickie my lad,' Old Walter offered generously. 'And I won't take it to heart or abandon the Spindlewood. I'll be as loyal as a sheepdog, you'll see.'

Richard winked at Jenny, then mock sighed heavily. 'Does that mean that you'll keep turning up on our doorstep every opening time and hog the bar all day and all night, like now?'

'So swipe me, Bob,' the old man said, holding up a hand in mock allegiance.

Richard shook his head sorrowfully. 'Pity. We were hoping we could shock you into abandoning us and plaguing the Three Feathers over in Bisley Bumpstead instead.'

This seemed to tickle the old man so much that he became almost purple-faced with laughter.

Jenny took the opportunity to slip off her stool and go to bed. It had been a long day.

* * *

The next morning dawned bright and sunny, with the forecast promising that the unusually hot days would continue well into next week. Jenny, rising at six in order to get the breakfast rolls made and proving in a warming drawer, hummed along to the radio as she worked.

Now that she knew more about the Sparkeys' hefty mortgage payments, she was more inclined to feel sympathetic to their money-grubbing ways. They might be brazen in squeezing every pound out of unsuspecting tourists now, but perhaps once they were free and clear of debt — and Celia Grimmett's old-fashioned edicts — they'd be able to relax a bit and enjoy themselves more.

Still humming to a golden oldie playing on the radio, she set the rice to boil for the kedgeree and began inspecting the eggs. So, omelettes — herb, tomato, or sausage? Or a mixture?

Jenny glanced up as a shadow moved across the light, and outside in the garden she saw the actress, Rachel, and a young man walking up the path. They chose to sit at a bench nearest to the paved patio area just outside the kitchen, and dumped their bags and things on the grass.

For a moment the cook wondered what they were doing there so early — and then she remembered that the am-dram players were due to give their second performance for the Regency weekenders right after breakfast. This time, it was to be a scene where Lady Hester and her lover meet for a romantic tryst. Lady Hester is to warn him that her husband has been threatening them, and he in turn attempts to persuade her to run away with him. But the thought of all that scandal would be too much for the timid and genteel lady.

Jenny was only glad that all the lovey-dovey acting didn't start until after everyone had eaten their food. No way did she want her eggs Benedict to be upstaged!

As she set about making the hollandaise for the eggs, she watched the two actors thoughtfully. 'Reginald Truby' looked to be in his mid-twenties, with fair hair and a rather square-chinned profile. He *was* rather good-looking, she mused wryly, so perhaps it was little wonder that am-dram had appealed to him. It probably gave him the ideal excuse to show off without looking too vain about it!

As she slowly whisked, drip by careful drip, some luscious and high-end oil into her egg yolks, Jenny realised that, far from rehearsing their upcoming scene, the two seemed to be arguing about something, with the young man's gestures becoming more and more angry and jerky. And, as the argument continued, Rachel's face began to get that mulish and sulky look that indicated that she was beginning to dig in her heels.

With a sigh, Jenny turned from the window and began to de-pip some fresh tomatoes. It was too early in the day for drama anyway — be it the real-life variety or strictly theatrical.

* * *

'I just can't stand spiders! They've always given me the horrors ever since I was a little girl. Isn't that right, Si?' Min Buckey looked up as Mags deposited a plate of gently steaming, fragrant kedgeree in front of her, and instantly the American woman beamed. 'Oh my, that looks good. It smells wonderful too.'

Jenny, sitting unobtrusively at a table for one tucked up almost inside the large inglenook fireplace, was indulging one of her favourite habits. Whenever possible, she liked to be present — and if possible incognito — when her food was being served, in order to get genuine feedback from her diners.

So this morning, once everything was prepared and ready, she had persuaded Muriel to let her into the dining room once the last dish had left the kitchen. As it happened, the American couple had been the last down, and so had been the last to give their order.

Now Jenny tucked happily into her own choice of herb omelette — just soft enough in the middle, but not runny — and checked for any signs of rubbery texture at the edges. Naturally, there were none. They wouldn't dare!

'Oh, Si, this *is* delicious,' Min gratifyingly murmured a moment later. 'You should have had this. Here, take a bite.'

Silas Buckey, Jenny noted, had chosen the French toast with a side order of bacon, but that didn't stop him from trying a forkful of his wife's dish.

'You're right, honey, it's great. I'll have it tomorrow,' he promised peaceably.

Jenny, continuing her survey of the dining room, wasn't surprised to see that Dr Gilchrist had opted for the croissants and her home-made apricot preserve. Ion, being slightly more adventurous, had chosen the sausage plait with mushrooms and grilled tomatoes.

'I just hope there won't be any spiders this morning,' again Min's rather loud voice, with its distinctive North Atlantic twang, cut across the room. 'Perhaps we should give the gardens a miss, honey,' she said worriedly. 'What do you think?'

'Well, Min, if we're going to look around the big house it seems a shame not to look at the gardens too. They're supposed to be really pretty,' her husband drawled back.

Jenny, recalling the itinerary for the weekend, remembered that after the breakfast 'show' the weekenders had the opportunity of either taking a tour of the local stately home, or visiting the local 'eyecatcher.' And she still hadn't found out what that was.

'Don't worry, Mrs Buckey — we don't have any poisonous spiders in England,' she heard Dr Gilchrist say as he leaned across his table to reassure the American, who was sitting at the table directly next to his.

'See, that's nice to know,' Silas said, reaching across to pat the top of his wife's hand comfortingly. 'Hear that, sweetie? There are no tarantulas or black widows over here!'

'Oh, Si, don't,' Min laughed and shuddered. Today the American matron was dressed in a loose-fitting pair of white slacks with another kaftan-style top, this one white and splashed with bright red and orange poppies. Red strappy sandals covered her small feet, and red chunky Bakelite bangles hung from one wrist.

'It's unlikely that you'll see any house spiders inside the big house either, Mrs Buckey. And garden spiders are quite pretty in their own way, a sort of brown and cream with a pretty pattern on their backs,' Rory Gilchrist added, no doubt trying to be helpful.

But Min merely blanched. 'Ugh. There simply can't possibly be anything pretty about a spider!' she argued with a laugh. 'But if you think it'll be all right in the house, well then, that's something. And, Si, sweetie, you can go around the gardens if you like. I'll stick to the buildings!'

'Whatever you say, honey,' her husband said again, barely pausing in his eating.

Several diners began to head off towards the loos, glancing at watches as they went, clearly making sure that they still had time before the show started.

Jenny, too, finished her cup of coffee and rose to her feet. Time to get back to the kitchen. It was the culinary highlight of the weekend that evening, and she was looking forward to getting started on the 'Regency Feast.' She hadn't ever cooked one before but she was up for the challenge.

As she made her way towards the side of the bar, she noticed the country solicitor, aka big bad Sir Hugh, standing behind the bar chatting earnestly to Muriel. Since the next scene concerned only Lady Hester and her young lover, he was dressed in civvies, and looked every inch the man of law.

She nodded vaguely at the landlady, but as she stepped through into the corridor, Rachel, in her full Lady Hester regalia, moved past her, and the cook quickly stepped out of her way, admiring the illusion she gave of a woman stepping two hundred years out of the past. But clearly visible on her wrist, Jenny noticed that the actress was wearing a very modern — and probably exorbitantly priced — platinum and diamond ladies' watch. She only hoped that the more eagle-eyed amongst the historical society contingent didn't spot it!

Behind her came Lady Hester's lover, the blond-haired Adonis of earlier, and this time Jenny got a good look at his rather fine green eyes. At the moment, however, the expression in them was far from pleasant. And they were boring into Rachel's back so hard, she was surprised not to see smoke coming from the back of the actress's sprigged-muslin outfit.

'Have you come to watch us, Vince? We're just going on,' Rachel called across to the older actor, who said something to Muriel in parting and then turned away.

'Coming,' Vince said brightly.

She noticed Rachel smile sweetly at Muriel and give her a mocking little wave.

'Don't think you've heard the last of this, Rae,' Jenny heard the Adonis hiss at Rachel's back. 'And don't think you can just shrug me off either!'

'Now then, you two, no more squabbling,' Jenny heard Vince say wearily, as she moved through to the kitchen. 'You've got a performance to put on. And, Rae, I think that reporter from the local paper might be in. So behave!'

Jenny smiled as she picked up her favourite apron from the back of a kitchen chair and slipped it over her clothes. It seemed that Vince, in role of peacemaker, was rather adept at handling his volatile fellow actors.

And rather him than her, she thought cheerfully, as she set about the first of her many tasks that day.

* * *

Half an hour later, Muriel watched her temporary cook carefully as Jenny set about making the dressing for her salad, which was to be one of the main centrepieces for that evening's make-or-break meal. Advertised in the brochure as the highlight of the weekend, the pressure was on for Jenny to get it right.

'And what's it called again?' Muriel asked, scowling down at the notebook in her hand. She was in charge of writing up the menus that would be placed on the tables, and had already picked out the 'old English' font she would use on her computer. But she wanted to make sure she got the spellings right.

'Salmagundi,' Jenny repeated patiently, and helpfully spelled it out for her. 'Apparently, it was a favourite salad with the Georgians, although it's much older than that, and consisted mainly of cooked chicken and hard-boiled eggs, romaine lettuce, with onions, anchovies, parsley, pickled red cabbage, green and red grapes, watercress, spinach and green beans.'

'Bloody hell,' Muriel muttered. 'I hope you haven't busted the food budget?'

Jenny assured her that she hadn't, and continued her lecture patiently. 'As with most dishes from the Georgian era, it has to presented in a rather spectacular manner, so I'm serving it on large platters, following a strict patterned arrangement, with edible flowers to top it all off,' Jenny swept on.

Adding wholegrain mustard, red wine vinegar, half a teaspoon of salt and ground pepper and a little olive oil to her dressing, she whisked it thoroughly. 'It's all in the preparation — first shred the lettuce and lay it on the platter, then cut the meat into thin slices and lay it on. Next comes a layer of sliced boiled eggs and onions, then the watercress, spinach, et cetera. All in progressively smaller layers, so you can see them all. Finally you decorate the top with the grapes and lemon slices and edible flowers. If done properly, it looks amazing and tastes great,' she enthused, getting carried away, as she always did, whenever she talked about food. 'It also has the added advantage of appealing to modern-day tastes because it's healthy for you!' And from her research she knew that not all Georgian recipes fell into *that* category!

Muriel nodded, looking pleased and a little less worried. She might not understand the intricacies and etiquette surrounding early nineteenth-century recipes, but she understood the importance of keeping her diners happy.

'And for the fish dish?'

'Ahh, fish is a bit of a problem area,' Jenny acknowledged. 'People living on the coast back then were OK — they could have fish fresh from the boats. But because they didn't have fridges in those days, and it could take days for carts to reach the more landlocked counties, most of the recipes for inland dwellers tended to be for freshwater fish caught locally — like pike.'

'Pike?' Muriel sounded appalled.

'Yes. It is rather bony, and not to everyone's taste,' Jenny agreed diplomatically. 'So, in the cause of authenticity, I've decided to go without a fish course,' she explained. 'But nobody will mind, I promise. Instead, there'll be a choice of Cornish game hens or boiled duck with onion sauce. And a veggie option, of course.'

'Boiled?' Muriel again sounded uncertain.

'I know it sounds strange to our ears, but believe me, it'll be delicious,' Jenny said firmly — and mentally crossed her fingers. Since she'd never boiled a duck before in her life, she was hoping that her confidence in the recipe wouldn't be misplaced. 'Those who know about these things will be well impressed,' she added slyly.

Seeing that Muriel still looked less than convinced, she swept on ruthlessly, 'And for dessert, there'll be a trifle, naturally. The Georgians did love their trifles — in my case I'm making Madeira cakes to go in the trifle, with blackcurrant jam, strawberries, raspberries and blackberries. Also on the dessert menu is something called a "whipt syllabub" — believe me, you don't want to know — with Shrewsbury cake, another must-have for a feast, apparently.' Jenny paused to take a much-needed breath. 'I've found a great recipe for them — they're actually more of a biscuit than a cake. Less crumbly than a shortbread, but with a great buttery flavour. They'll be perfect with the syllabub, trust me.'

Muriel, wisely deciding that she should just leave her to get on with it, made sure that she had all the information she needed to print off the menus and left. Jenny watched her go, heaved a sigh of relief, then glanced at her watch.

Just gone ten o'clock. Since she needed some sherry to soak some raisins in, she went through to the bar just as the diners and actors began pouring out of the dining room, happily chatting about the scene they'd just witnessed. And from the flush of triumph on Rachel's face, she'd clearly been a hit yet again.

'Rae, I need a word,' her handsome co-star said, taking her arm and attempting to pull her off to one corner for some privacy. Clearly Rachel Norman wasn't enamoured with that idea because she angrily jerked her arm away.

'Not now, Matt! I need to go and speak to the reporter . . .'

'That can wait! You don't seem to realise that Felicity has actually broken off our engagement,' he hissed.

'Well that's not my fault is it,' Rachel hissed back. 'You should have been more careful and made sure that she didn't find out about us. Good grief, other men manage to do it! In any case, it was only ever going to be just a bit of a laugh between us anyway, wasn't it? It's not as if it was anything serious that she needed to get her knickers in a twist over! Just win her back if you're so damned keen to marry her. Personally, I think you're better off without the silly little . . . Silas, sweetie, what did you think of my performance!'

And turning her back firmly on Matthew's thunderous face, she beamed at the wealthy American and glided across towards him. And Jenny didn't blame Min one bit for the way she moved protectively closer to her husband and reached out to slip her hand under his arm and give it an affectionate squeeze.

No doubt, Jenny thought cynically, Rachel had now had time to learn (as Jenny had) that Silas had recently sold his businesses and thus must now be rolling in ready money — and might just be on the lookout for a pretty woman to help him spend some of it.

And as Jenny had seen for herself, the actress had plenty of expensive tastes. Neither the jewellery nor clothes that she favoured were of the cheap variety.

'Richard — I need a bottle of good sherry please,' Jenny said, turning to the bar and reminding herself firmly that she had work to do.

'Why? A secret tippler, are you?' he asked with an uncertain grin.

Jenny shook her head. 'Don't worry, sherry's not my drink,' she reassured him. 'Actually, forget the bottle, I really only need a little shot-glass full — about so much,' she said, using her finger and thumb to show about an inch or two of space. 'Just enough to soak some raisins and sultanas.'

Ignoring his obvious trust issues, she instead nodded across at the pretty actress who was now clearly flirting with a delighted Silas. 'She looks like she's after a rich sugar daddy,' she said lightly. 'Or does she already come from money?'

Richard snorted. 'Not her! Her mum and dad still live on one of the council estates in Gloucester. And she works as a secretary at some local haulage firm. Where, no doubt, she has all the tough lorry drivers wrapped around her little finger,' he predicted bitterly. He shook his head as he glowered across at the actress. 'Those Americans had better watch out for her. She'll cause trouble there, you mark my words!'

And so saying, he poured her a small glass of sherry and then moved off down the bar, to where Old Walter was tapping his empty beer glass significantly.

Jenny, surprised by the unexpected bitterness of Richard's comments, began to feel the first stirrings of uneasiness. It was definitely beginning to feel as if there were some nasty undercurrents swirling at the Spindlewood Inn this weekend. And wanting no part in them, Jenny grabbed her glass of sherry and was about to turn back to her kitchen when Dr Gilchrist, coming past her, almost jogged her arm.

Luckily, Jenny was adept at saving her ingredients, and managed to keep her sherry in the glass.

'Oh I'm so sorry,' the Oxford don apologised, noticing her deft avoidance tactics. 'I'm not usually that clumsy.'

'It's OK,' Jenny said. Then, catching him eyeing her glass of sherry with a look of surprise, forced herself to laugh. 'Don't worry — I'm not hitting the hard stuff early. It's for cooking purposes only, I swear. I'm the cook,' she introduced herself.

'So we have you to thank for all the wonderful food?'
Jenny beamed.

'I'm really looking forward to tonight's feast,' the Oxford man swept on. 'Truth is, it's one of the main reasons why I joined up for this shindig. The food at High Table is all well and good, but occasionally a man needs to stretch his culinary repertoire a bit. And the Regency banquet caught my eye. I'm not really into all the melodrama, personally,' he swept a hand around, indicating the costumed theatricals around him. 'But I thought I might enjoy the food, and perhaps write an article for one of the academic journals that I write for about the local eyecatcher.'

Jenny was about to ask him exactly what that was, when he added quickly, 'Oh, there's Vince. Sorry, but I need a word with him. Do excuse me.' And before she could so much as utter another word, he darted away.

Jenny noticed that the Welshman, Ion Dryfuss, who had been talking to the solicitor, moved aside to make way for him, and went over to a window seat instead, where he sat down moodily. And once again, he began watching Rachel Norman intently.

And fighting back yet another little shiver of foreboding at the dark emotion that was clearly apparent on his triangular-shaped and arresting face, Jenny escaped gratefully back to the sanctuary of her kitchen.

CHAPTER FOUR

It was lovely to hear the inn finally fall silent for a while as everyone set out to enjoy his or her various excursions. With only Old Walter left behind, propping up the bar in his usual place, and with the occasional, non-Regency customer coming in for drinks and lunch, Jenny was left in relative peace.

Muriel, along with Mags and Babs, was on hand to oversee the few lunch orders they received, leaving her free to concentrate on her masterpiece. Although she'd spoken with confidence about her boiled duck dish, Jenny had to admit to feeling a little trepidation at trying out a new recipe without having had the luxury of doing a trial run first.

Outside, it was another glorious day. And at three o'clock, with everything ticking over nicely, she took a short break from the hot kitchen and went through to the bar to thirstily order a large lemon and lime with lots of ice from Richard.

As she accepted the glass, tinkling melodiously with ice cubes, she ignored Old Walter — who was trying to catch her eye — and instead took her drink to one of the comfortable padded window seats. As she settled herself down however, she noticed that a curious-looking lump of white material had been tossed casually on the other end of the seat.

It seemed to be made of silk, a material known for its sinuous pliability, and yet it looked, paradoxically, rather rigid. Intrigued, Jenny reached across and fingered it, and then saw the rows of eyelets and strings, ribbed and rigid panels, and quickly realised what it was.

An old-fashioned corset!

For a moment, as the Junoesque cook examined it thoughtfully, she could only reflect that she was glad she hadn't been born in an era when a woman with her curves would have been required to wear such an instrument of torture.

She supposed, idly, that the corset must belong to Rachel and was probably a part of her costume, and that the actress must have left it here and then forgotten about it — perhaps after being distracted by one of her many suitors.

But then, just as quickly, she dismissed the idea. Rachel was naturally slender, and Jenny was sure — the few times that she'd seen the actress in costume — that she hadn't been wearing a garment like this.

Then who . . . Jenny sighed. Of course — it had to belong to Min. Her costume, being far more Victorian in appearance, would definitely benefit from a garment like this. And, Jenny supposed with a little pang of sympathy mixed with chagrin, that the American woman might, given the advent of Rachel on the scene, now be feeling just a little bit insecure about her more middle-aged figure. Although not fat, she certainly didn't possess a figure as svelte as that of the actress.

With a sad little sigh, she turned her attention away from the corset and sipped her cold drink with pleasure, glancing around absently as she did so. The inn really was a lovely place, she thought, and she could well understand why Richard and Muriel had coveted it, and had been willing to take on such an unusual mortgage agreement in order to own it.

As she glanced out the window and observed the attractive village square, Ion Dryfuss walked in through the open door, looking cool and elegant in black trousers and a loose-fitting white shirt. He was carrying a large artist's folder under his arm in which, she supposed, he'd placed his latest efforts at brass rubbing.

He ordered a lager at the bar, spotted her, visibly hesitated for a moment or two, and then, realising that ignoring her now might appear rude, smiled and sat down at the table next to her. 'Hello. Are you here for the Regency do?' he asked conversationally.

'Only to cook for it,' Jenny admitted, and introduced herself. Then she nodded at the portfolio. 'Brass rubbings? I overheard you talking about them to Muriel when you first arrived,' she explained, when he shot her a surprised look. 'Can I see them?' Not that she was particularly interested in such an esoteric activity, but the handsome and rather enigmatic young man intrigued her. And besides, she could listen to his sing-song Welsh-valleys voice all day long!

'If you like,' he offered with a shrug, and passed the folder over. 'There are some nice pieces from the old crusader's sarcophagus in the local church here.'

'Oh. Are they the ones that usually have an effigy of a little faithful dog at their feet?' she asked, turning over the pages of black crayon markings.

'Usually,' Ion laughed. Then suddenly he tensed as Jenny turned a page and saw not a brass rubbing at all, but a proper sketch. Drawn freehand and obviously the work of a talented amateur, it showed a woman in side profile, with her hair blowing beguilingly in the wind.

It was the face of Rachel Norman.

Beside her, Jenny heard him draw in his breath sharply, and in her peripheral vision could tell that he'd gone rigid and slightly pale.

'That's rather a good likeness,' Jenny said casually, pretending not to notice her companion's obvious unhappiness over the fact that she'd seen it. Clearly, he'd forgotten that it was in the folder. 'She's rather lovely, isn't she?' Jenny added nonchalantly.

'Er . . . yes. We met earlier this summer. She was on holiday in North Wales and I was working in a bar on the esplanade,' he offered a shade unwillingly.

Jenny smiled. 'That's nice,' she said vaguely. And much to his relief, closed the folder and handed it back to him. 'Well, I've got to get back to the kitchen. An authentic Regency feast won't cook itself.'

'I'm sure it'll be wonderful,' Ion predicted chivalrously, looking almost comically relieved that she'd paid so little attention to his etchings. 'The food's been smashing so far,' he flattered her eagerly.

Jenny beamed at the compliment, and went back to the kitchen. But as she did so, she couldn't help but wonder why he'd felt so rattled. Clearly Ion and Rachel had had a summer fling earlier in the year, a holiday romance, which at last put paid to any lingering question hovering over the foxy-faced Welshman's sexuality.

But presumably the fling had then gone the way of all summer romances, and hadn't survived. As far as it went, the story was sad, perhaps, but all rather boringly normal nevertheless.

But why had he then followed her back to her home territory, here in the Cotswolds? Didn't that smack a little of stalking? Presumably Rachel must have noticed his presence — and yet she couldn't recall seeing the actress actually talking to him, or even acknowledging his presence. But that meant nothing — for all Jenny knew, they could have got together anywhere, anytime, and had any number of intimate conversations.

And considering that Rachel had, at some point, also been involved with that good-looking, fair-haired Adonis, Matthew (to the extent, it would seem, of ruining his engagement to another woman), she doubted that Ion could be feeling very happy right now. For he could hardly have failed to see all the pointers indicating that Rachel was searching for yet another romance.

Richard Sparkey couldn't have been the only one aware of her pursuit of the rich American, when he'd so grimly predicted that Rachel was about to upset another long-standing relationship.

And given her new employer's bitterness on the subject of Rachel, it made her wonder if perhaps, at some point, Rachel might not have caused some friction in the Sparkeys' own marriage?

Shaking her head — and reminding herself yet again that such speculation was none of her business — Jenny went to make sure the trifles were behaving themselves and setting properly. Naturally, they were.

But should she have gone with the 'fricandeau of veal' or the 'curry of rabbit' instead of the boiled duck?

* * *

By six o'clock that evening, all the guests were back from their various sightseeing trips, and were chatting happily over drinks at the bar.

Listening with only half an ear to their chatter as it wafted through the door, Jenny absently learned that Min had remained thankfully unmolested by spiders whilst visiting the country house and gardens, Vince and Rory Gilchrist had been much taken with the eyecatcher (still a mystery to Jenny), and the visit to the graves of the original Lady Hester and Reginald Truby had been variously touching, sad, and romantic.

Jenny, frantically making sure that every sauce was reducing properly, that the salad was ready to be constructed, and that everything that needed to be chilled was being chilled, paid scant attention to any of it.

Muriel hurried in and out, anxiously checking on her progress in between making sure that the dining room was a mass of arranged flowers and all the best 'bib and tucker' was on display, giving the cosy room as much of an air of grandeur as possible.

In short, it was organised chaos.

'I only hope they all opt for the more expensive wines,' she heard the landlady muttering under her breath as she shot past Jenny with a basket full of their best silver.

Jenny grinned and hoped they did too — if not for quite the same reason. Muriel might want to make a huge profit on the wine, but Jenny only wanted the best drinks possible to complement all this magnificent food that she'd so lovingly slaved over all day!

* * *

Dinner was due to start at seven-thirty, and would be a full six courses — modest by Regency standards, but far more manageable for twenty-first-century tastes. With a quarter of an hour to go, Mags and Babs were girding their collective loins in the kitchen, whilst Jenny, now that the moment of truth was upon her, felt curiously calm.

The duck was going to be wonderful.

Her salads, heaped on blue-and-white platters, looked spectacular.

Her trifles and syllabub were going to be a sensation.

She was standing in the open doorway of the kitchen, benevolently taking in the mass of happy, expectant and chattering people crammed into the bar beyond. Once again, everyone who had a costume was dressed in all their bedazzling glory. Behind the bar, Richard was encouraging guests to try the brandy and cognac and an aged Marsala that he'd 'ordered in, special.' Old Walter, eyes agog at all the fuss and to-do, watched the spectacle happily, hopeful that someone would offer to buy him an expensive 'short' too.

Nearest to her stood Rachel, dressed now in a beautiful pearl-grey silk ensemble topped with an ostrich-feather hair ornament, looking every inch as if she should be in a ballroom in Bath somewhere in the year 1814, fighting off various young 'bucks' who wanted to fill up her dance card. Beside her, her 'husband' Sir Hugh stood sipping appreciatively on one of Richard's cognacs.

'Nervous?' Vince asked her.

Rachel laughed and shook her head. 'Of course not. Mind you, Matthew's looking a bit green around the gills. I hope he's learned his lines properly this time.'

Jenny looked, and sure enough, saw that the fair-haired Adonis, now dressed like a Regency Beau Brummell in cream silk trousers, ornately embroidered silver-and-gold waistcoat and green velvet jacket, did look rather nervous.

'He better have,' the country solicitor said ominously. 'After fluffing his lines in *An Inspector Calls* last year, the committee will downgrade him to non-speaking parts otherwise,' he predicted ominously.

But clearly Rachel wasn't interested in the woes of her fellow am-dram actors. 'Vince, you're a solicitor, right,' she said, her husky voice rising in volume a notch or two.

'Last time I looked, yes,' the older man agreed mockingly.

'So if you know somebody's been doing something . . . naughty . . . can you get in trouble if you don't tell the police?' she asked.

At this, Jenny looked at her sharply, as did her companion, and, Jenny noticed, a rather good-looking woman sitting a little further down the bar. In her early forties, she wasn't dressed in costume but a rather nice trouser suit in navy blue, which suited her pale complexion, red hair and dark blue eyes.

Jenny noticed that this intriguing question had also caught the ear of Richard, who as usual was serving behind the bar and had now begun moving slowly their way, his ears no doubt straining. And who could blame him? The question had definitely been a conversation-stopper.

And Rachel was making no effort to keep her voice down.

Vince began to look slightly concerned. 'If you're aware of a crime then it's your duty to report it to the police, yes,' he said firmly — as any good, respectable solicitor might. 'But you'd need to consider the circumstances most carefully,' he then temporised. Which again, was typical of a solicitor. 'You'd have to be sure of your grounds, if making a specific accusation against someone. The laws of slander and libel aren't to be taken lightly. But if you have knowledge of a crime then yes, you need to report it.'

'Hmmm . . .' Rachel said. Then sighed. 'I suppose you can be had up for being an accessory or something if you don't, can't you? Accessory after the fact, or whatever they call it?'

'That is the case if you're aware a crime has been committed and don't report it,' Vince corrected her. 'If you're aware that a crime is going to occur and don't report it, then you're an accessory before the fact. Either way, there can be severe penalties. It depends what it is you know, and what the crime is. Look, Rachel,' Vince said sharply, 'if you're in any doubt about this, you need to do something about it. I can advise you if you want to come and see me in my office. I can also accompany you when you speak to the police if you think you might need legal representation.'

At this point, Rachel smiled and waved a hand vaguely in the air. 'Oh no, Vince, I don't think I'll need to take you up on that. Anyway, it was more of a rhetorical question,' she laughed lightly. 'It's probably nothing anyway. I think it's just easier to say nothing . . . Just forget I said anything. It's such a piffling thing anyway — probably not even a crime as such at all, so it's hardly worth the effort,' she rattled on with a dismissive shrug.

'Now look, Rachel . . .'

'Vince, honestly, it's nothing,' she flicked a hand in the air and gave him an impish smile. 'I promise! Now, let's concentrate on the matter at hand shall we? Are you ready to go and slap the old glove in Matthew's face and challenge him to a duel?'

Vince clearly wanted to ask her more about her 'hypothetical' question, but didn't get the chance. For as she began to make her way into the middle of the room, she began delivering her opening lines to Reginald Truby, thus indicating to their audience that the next performance was about to begin.

After that everyone would dine, and after that there'd be a final confrontation scene between the star-crossed lovers and the angry husband, which would culminate in the duel tomorrow morning.

Jenny, mindful that she needed to start overseeing the plating up of the starters and soups, dashed back into the kitchen. And for the next few hours, she promptly forgot about everything but ensuring that every plate that left her kitchen was perfection.

* * *

Jenny was feeling a shade frazzled some three hours later, when she decided to venture into the dining room only as the final scene of the evening was being played out, and all her wonderful Regency recipes had now been safely served and consumed. As she passed from her kitchen across the narrow corridor and into the bar, she noticed that Dr Gilchrist, alone in the assembly, had decided to forgo watching the dramatics. Instead, he was seated at a small table for two tucked away in a corner of the bar lounge, talking to the fetching redhead in the trouser suit that Jenny had noticed earlier.

Just a quick glance in passing told her that they were talking earnestly and ferociously, heads bent close together, and neither of them looked happy. In fact, they were not so much talking as hissing at one another, and the Oxford don had a look of haunted fury about him, whilst his companion's face was white with spite.

Hastily passing them by (the travelling cook had no interest in listening to anyone's private spats), she stood in the archway to the dining room, careful to stay in the shadows and not be a distraction as the 'challenge to the duel' scene was played out in front of her.

With a sense of vague curiosity, if not much interest, Jenny watched the various performances — and decided that of the three of them, it was probably the country solicitor who was the most natural actor. Rachel depended far too heavily on her looks and that amazing voice of hers, and as a result sometimes came off as rather 'hammy' or stiff. Her one-time ex-lover, Jenny was amused to note, didn't forget a single line, and as the young lover, Reginald, came across as a decent enough romantic lead. He certainly had the looks for it. But his performance was patchy, and it seemed to her that his mind wasn't wholly on the job at hand.

Whereas the country solicitor was obviously having a grand old time as the 'big, bad Sir Hugh' and played him with a mixture of gusto and glee that struck a chord with his audience.

But at the end of the scene all three got an enthusiastic round of applause, and were quickly surrounded by well-wishers, eager to thank them and talk about the 'real' duel that had taken place centuries ago.

Behind her, Jenny heard a sharp sound and turned to see that the red-headed woman had slammed down her glass on the table and was now thrusting back her chair, causing it to scrape loudly across the original oak floorboards. The next moment, she was storming off in high dudgeon.

In his seat, Rory Gilchrist watched her go, his face grim.

'Well, I think that went well,' Jenny heard Vince say behind her, and quickly stepped aside as the happy guests and actors began the short trek from the dining room to descend on the bar en masse. And as they passed, Jenny was very pleased to note that a good percentage of the diners were commenting on the Regency feast as much as the amateur dramatics.

'Who'd have thought boiled duck would be so delicious?' pleased her, as did, 'I have no idea what those Shrewsbury cakes were, but I wish I had the recipe.'

Still basking in reflected glory, she made her way over to where Muriel was overseeing Mags and Babs as they began setting everything straight, ready for tomorrow's breakfast.

'Everyone seems to have enjoyed the food,' Jenny said pointedly, just in case her employer had missed that vital fact.

'Hmmm? Yes, yes, so they did,' Muriel said vaguely, confirming the cook's fears that her employer's mind was obviously engaged elsewhere. 'Well done, Jenny,' she added as a distinct afterthought, and with that, began to gather up a tray of coffee cups. When she'd finished helping them out, Jenny made her way to the bar and patiently waited her turn at the back. When she'd finally caught the barmaid's eye, she ordered a celebratory glass of white wine and retired to an unobtrusive spot by the fireplace — unlit now, given the late-summer heat wave — and sat down for a well-earned rest.

Her feet were throbbing slightly since she'd been on them all day, but she felt, overall, a pleasant and relaxed glow settle over her. As she sipped her wine contentedly, her eyes roamed around the room. And the cook finally admitted to herself that, in spite of her bout of self-congratulation, she was beginning to feel distinctly nervous about the way this weekend seemed to be going.

In the past, Jenny had had the misfortune of being present when something decidedly nasty and fatal had occurred. And for the last twenty-four hours or so, she had been trying to convince herself that lightning couldn't possibly be about to strike again.

But she was failing miserably.

There were obvious tensions roiling around — some of them centring around Rachel, certainly, but others around Rory Gilchrist and his acrimonious lady friend. Then there were the wealthy Americans (and where there was money there was always trouble) — and she was even beginning to think that there was something going on with Vince. Solicitors, in Jenny's view, could be magnates for all sorts of legal trouble.

But that didn't necessarily mean that anything bad was going to happen, she told herself firmly. You could take any diverse assembly of people, and human nature being what it was, you were bound to have friction.

She had just been unlucky in the past when that friction had turned murderous, that was all. She was just being silly in feeling so uneasy.

That being said, Jenny made the decision that come tomorrow morning, when everybody filed out to the nearby farmer's field to watch the 'duel,' she would stay very firmly — not to mention *safely* — behind and in her kitchen.

Jenny Starling was no mug!

For the thought of a firearm — even a theatrical prop — being bandied about and fired was enough to give any would-be murderer ideas. And if it did, she wanted to be far away and well out of it all. That way, if anything untoward *did* occur during the duel, no police officer would have any recourse to interview *her* or look at her with suspicious eyes.

Which would make a nice change.

Having decided that to her satisfaction, Jenny continued to sip her wine and forced herself to relax.

She noticed that Rory Gilchrist had buttonholed Vince again, and that the two of them were talking intently.

Hastily, she turned her eyes away. None of her business, she reminded herself firmly. She took a last swallow of her wine and then headed determinedly towards the bar to deposit her glass.

As she did so, she passed a small knot of people gathered to one side, and heard Rachel's distinctive voice.

'Wasn't Matthew great, Ion?'

Jenny sighed.

'Yes — not that I'm the one to ask,' she heard that lovely Welsh-valleys voice reply. 'I don't get to the theatre that often.'

'Poor you. Matthew and I often used to go, didn't we?' Rachel purred. 'Well we would, wouldn't we, so that we could pick up pointers. Did I tell you, Matt, that I'm having a new portfolio done with that marvellous photographer Julius Bristow recommended?'

'What, the chap in Soho? The one who does all the television stars? Isn't he really expensive?'

Jenny glanced across in time to see Rachel laugh and put a hand on Matthew's arm.

'Of course he is, but he's well worth it. Ion would agree with me — he always said the camera loves me. Remember all the photos you took of me back in May?' Rachel shot an amused glance at the Welshman, then back at her blond-haired companion. Not surprisingly the two jilted lovers were shooting daggers at each other.

'I'm surprised you can afford it on your pay,' Matthew said spitefully. 'Still signing the lorries out and counting them back in are you?' he added with a sweet smile.

But instead of replying sharply, as she'd expected Rachel would do at this obvious attempt to put her down, Jenny noticed that her gaze had gone beyond Matthew's shoulder and seemed to rest thoughtfully on someone else. And a bright smile suddenly lit her face.

'Oh, I don't mind secretarial work,' she said, her deep sexy voice rising in volume again. 'It's only temporary after all, until I get a part in the commercials again. My agent says he can really build on that. He confidently expects I'll be getting small television parts before next Christmas. So I won't be working in an office for long. Besides, there are compensations. All those lovely muscular lorry drivers, for example.'

At this both men stiffened, and Jenny shook her head. Rachel was clearly a woman who liked playing with fire.

'You know, not all of them are forty with beer guts and ridiculous tattoos. Some of them are quite buff,' Rachel swept on with a knowing and enthusiastic smile. 'Of course, some of them can be bad boys too. You know, a bit rough around the edges. Our boss, well, let's just say that he doesn't always do the proper background checks that he should. I wouldn't be surprised if one or two of our drivers hadn't been a guest of her Majesty at some point or other, if you know what I mean.'

'That doesn't sound safe,' Ion said, sounding genuinely alarmed. 'Rachel, have any of them tried anything on with you?'

But Rachel laughed off this chivalrous concern. 'Oh, don't you worry about me,' she assured him loftily, 'all us girls like the bad boys! They're so sexy. But most of us have the good sense to keep them at arm's length. Mind you, that doesn't stop a girl from flirting with them now and then and learning all their little secrets. Men are so easy, aren't they? They just love talking about themselves. I've never met a man yet who didn't think he was fascinating.'

54

And again, although she was looking in Matthew's direction, Jenny had the feeling her voice was definitely directed elsewhere. The cook shifted her position slightly, trying to see who the actress had in mind.

Behind Matthew, Jenny could see Silas and Min were standing close together, drinking out of bulbous glasses of brandy in amicable harmony. Just beyond them sat Rory and Vince, still in earnest conversation, although she rather thought that Vince was paying more attention to what Rachel was saying than his old friend. Jenny watched as Muriel offered them both a refill of their glasses and was abruptly waved away.

'Anyway, I have more sense than to get involved with truckers, no matter how naughty and good-looking they are,' Rachel said flippantly, and with a wave of dismissal, firmly changed the subject. 'Now, which of you two boys wants to buy me one of those ruinously expensive cognacs Richard is so keen to push?'

Jenny set off towards her kitchen to see for herself just what state Mags and Babs had left it in after all that washing up and clearing away. Women who liked to set men at each other's throats, just for the fun of watching them fight over her, had never been amongst Jenny's favourite people.

CHAPTER FIVE

Sunday lunch was served promptly at one o'clock and offered a traditional choice of roast beef, chicken, lamb or pork, all served with the obligatory accompaniment of roast potatoes, vegetables, stuffing and sauces. A variety of fruit crumbles and some rather more exotic options were on offer for dessert.

Contrary to all her pessimistic fears, Jenny, feeling rather abashed, had quickly learned that nothing out of the ordinary — let alone dangerous — had transpired at the dawn duel. Unless you counted the fact that Matthew, who couldn't ride very well, had nearly fallen off his horse when riding up to meet Sir Hugh under the old oak.

The fake shot had been fired from the replica pistol without incident. And after Reginald Truby had been so foully done to death, and Sir Hugh had departed in disgrace, Matthew Greenslade had then got up from his prone position on the grass to take a bow, and everyone had returned to the inn in high spirits.

Once again, everyone was dressed in costume as they enjoyed their meal, because right afterwards the final 'suicide' scene was to be enacted at the village pond. Or lake, rather, Jenny mentally corrected herself with a grin.

And not wanting to be such a killjoy again, she was going to go with the others to watch Rachel's big scene. It wasn't very often, after all, that you got the chance to watch a Regency maiden kill herself to very dramatic effect on a lovely late summer's afternoon in the Cotswolds, was it?

So immediately after lunch was over, Jenny went upstairs to take a quick shower and change. It was as she was pulling on a light floral skirt in various rainbow hues that she heard angry raised voices coming through the thin partition wall, and felt a definite sense of déjà vu as she once again heard Rachel Norman's voice. But then she felt a distinct jolt of surprise when, instead of hearing one of her fellow actors' voices answering her back, she instead heard a distinctly American voice, also raised in anger.

'You clearly can't see that you're beginning to make poor Si feel downright embarrassed,' she heard Min Buckey say tightly. 'What's more, young lady, you're starting to make a complete fool of yourself as well.'

Jenny reached for the first blouse she could find and hastily began buttoning it up.

'Really?' she heard Rachel's voice drawling sardonically in reply. 'Well, I can't say as I've seen him objecting much,' she jeered. 'In fact, from what he's said, he seemed to imply that it was rather nice having someone take notice of him for a change. Been neglecting him a bit have we? I hear that can happen when you've been married for too long. The poor dears do so like to have their ego stroked, don't they?'

Jenny quickly slipped her feet into a pair of light tan sandals.

'No I have not been neglecting him!' the American matron screeched. 'And I don't believe a word of what you're saying. Si told me only last night that he thought you were coming on a bit strong. Poor baby was even blushing. You were hanging on to his arm like a limpet all last night. But it won't do you any good you know. How dumb do you think we are, honey? A man has money, and he attracts the likes of you like wasps around a jam pot.' Min laughed nastily. 'Do you really think you're the first young bit of stuff to try it on with Silas? But he's wise to you. You girls are all alike — you see a middle-aged man and think he's a fool, and that you can just . . .'

Jenny grabbed her bag and headed for the door. Whilst her sympathies were fully with Min, she had no desire to hear any more. Not that she couldn't help but hear the last few sentences of the American woman's bitter words as she slipped out the door and headed off down the corridor.

'. . . this time tomorrow, me and Si will be in Stratford-upon-Avon, having a high old time, and he'll already have forgotten what you look like. So don't think you'll be wangling anything out of him, any little bits of jewellery as a parting gift or . . .'

Jenny headed rapidly down the rather narrow upper set of stairs and smiled blandly at Vincent as he passed her coming up the other way. No doubt he was intent on going to the changing rooms to get out of his costume. She hesitated, wondering whether she should warn him that he might be about to walk in on a rather nasty little scene of quite a different kind, but decided it wasn't her place.

Besides, hopefully his appearance would bring the argument between the two women to a quick end.

Back down in the bar, Jenny glanced at the clock and realised that it was nearly three o'clock already, and that everyone was gathered together, eager to follow the tragic Lady Hester as she made her final journey. As well as all the members of the historical society, Jenny gauged that a fair few of the villagers had also turned out, no doubt attracted by the Regency Extravaganza's recent activities, and all keen to watch as a young woman dramatically drowned herself for love.

Jenny saw Min sweep into the room a few minutes after she did, looking both flushed and satisfied. Clearly, she felt better for getting things off her impressive chest, and Jenny felt like applauding her. The American woman was again wearing her Victorian-era tea-gown, which sat on her plump figure most becomingly, and Jenny was glad to see that she hadn't forced her figure into her corset this time.

The cook saw Min's husband go across and greet her, and clearly say something complimentary about her hair, for Min immediately reached up a hand to pat her elaborate wig and gave a laugh and a nod.

Dressed in his own costume, he looked faintly ridiculous in his silks and cravat, but it was somehow touching to see that he was prepared to get into the spirit of the thing for her sake. For Jenny had no doubt that the whole dress-up aspect of the Regency weekend had been Min's idea.

Vince came back down a few minutes later, now dressed in casual grey slacks and a white shirt. Behind the bar, Richard — dressed in his 'peasant' smock outfit complete with the comical floppy hat that fell over his ears and forehead and must surely have severely limited his line of vision — was busy calling last orders and trying to push the last of his expensive spirits. By his side, Muriel poured a glass of brandy for someone dressed as a country parson, then nodded to her husband as he passed behind her, leaving her to finish up serving the last of the stragglers alone. It wouldn't do for them to be serving alcohol all day on a Sunday.

Ion was patiently waiting for the show to begin, and was sitting over on one of the window seats, but there was no sign of his rival-in-love Matthew, Jenny noticed, with some relief. So at least there would be no more trouble there. But when she thought about it, it was obvious why the blond-haired Adonis was nowhere in sight. As the now dead Reginald Truby, his presence would have been definitely inappropriate and might have spoiled the effect for the rest of the audience. After all, Rachel was about to kill herself over his loss, and it would strain anyone's ability to believe in her dramatic gesture if the man she was about to kill herself over was standing right there in the wings, watching her!

Behind the bar, Richard once again took over from his wife and Muriel hurried out into the kitchen with a tray full of empty glasses. Jenny had a vague memory of Patsy telling her that the pub was usually closed on a Sunday — probably something to do with satisfying the clauses in Celia Grimmett's conditions for the conversion of the dwelling into the inn. Naturally though, when the Sparkeys played host to weekend guests, that rule had to be suspended.

A hush fell across the room, and Jenny looked up as a tall, imposing figure dressed uncompromisingly all in black swept through and into the lounge. She heard one or two small gasps of surprise and approval ripple around her, for the figure moving silently across the room was undeniably an eye-catching one — and definitely rather spooky.

Jenny wasn't sure if Regency women actually dressed in head-to-toe black when they were bereaved. Surely that had become popular in Queen Victoria's time?

But it seemed a rather petty quibble under the circumstances, for the dramatic figure in black was certainly something to see — not least because she wore a full black veil over her face. Her dress was made of black silk and lace and fell straight to the floor, obscuring the actress's feet, making it appear as if she was gliding rather than walking. This, in turn, had the effect of making the audience feel as if she were already dead, and that they were already watching her ghost drift mournfully by.

She was wearing long black gloves that clutched her black beaded reticule tightly, and if her movements were a little jerky and self-conscious, it hardly mattered, given the overall effect.

And then she began her final speech, and her wonderfully smoky, deep, sexy voice filled the room, throbbing with emotion, and any uneasy fears her audience had that Rachel's performance might just let her down were immediately lifted.

'Oh, my lover has gone, and I am bereft,' she began, lifting a hand to her forehead and pressing the opaque black covering of her veil theatrically against her skin. 'And am I truly destined to carry on so cruelly living whilst all my sensibilities tell me that to do so would be futile?'

And so, lamenting and bewailing her loss, Rachel Norman made her way to the door and out into the bright

— and definitely incongruous — sunshine, trailing her eager retinue of listeners behind her. To the slight consternation of a dog walker and a pair of local teenagers, who all turned their heads to stare at her as she passed them by, she led the way slowly across the village square. In one corner there was a small gate that led onto a piece of common ground, which contained a well-worn footpath that swept down to the village pond.

In several places, Rachel would pause to allow everyone to catch up with her, whilst lamenting some more. And all the time working herself up to 'commit such a dread deed, which although must be deemed unpardonable in the eyes of God, is surely not past understanding to my fellow man.'

Jenny, who was towards the back of the crowd, was clearly able to hear her words carrying on the still, open air, and once again had to admire her delivery. That marvellous and unmistakable voice of hers really did manage to convey the anguish of a woman about to end her life, working up her courage and her conviction to join her beloved 'beyond the veil.'

So much so that by the time the procession had reached the rather pretty village pond, everyone was perfectly willing to believe that they were, in fact, on the shores of the small ornamental lake that still existed within the grounds of the Rowland family home. (The Rowlands, it seemed, whilst not minding taking money from the weekenders to look around their house and garden, hadn't been quite so eager to lend their lake to this afternoon's proceedings.)

As Jenny and the others formed a large semicircle around the front of the pond, the cook looked around her with interest. A waist-high wire fence, colonised by pink and white flowering bindweed and other wildflowers, met the pond at a point halfway across its circumference, and circled it around the back, thus cutting off the rear of the pond from public access. No doubt the farmer's field behind it was used for pasture, and the village committee didn't want cows or sheep polluting the water, trampling down the vegetation and ruining the aspect.

Covering up most of the fencing was a row of elegantly weeping willows that lined two thirds of the pond, their feathery green branches sweeping down clear to the water, creating a natural, lushly green theatrical curtain as a backdrop. Bullrushes and other varieties of native reeds rustled gently in the breeze, their tall stems making inroads into various other parts of the water, leaving a relatively clear patch of open water only in the very centre of the pond. But even here, some late-flowering pondweed with pretty star-like yellow flowers presented a lovely splash of colour, as did the waving lime-green weeds that lay just below the surface of the smooth water.

Dragon and damsel flies flitted away at the disturbance, flashing their electric-blue and green slender bodies as they did so, and a family of moorhens sped away in panic to the far side of the pond, as far away from the human invasion as possible.

A rather picturesque, rickety-looking jetty stretched out almost to the centre of the pond. The main wooden posts supporting the planks rose to about eight inches or so above the waterline. Jenny suspected the youngsters of the village used it the most, since it would allow them to get further out onto the water to feed the ducks, which were thankfully absent right now.

Jenny, hiding a smile, thought that it would rather spoil the sombre mood if some mallards came quacking up to Rachel during her big scene, demanding to be fed some bread!

As it was, a gentle late summer's breeze wafted a few meadow brown butterflies across the scene as Rachel walked to the water's edge and began her final, farewell speech.

'And so, I pray that Reginald now awaits me, confident that God, in his infinite grace, will grant me forgiveness and look down with mercy on my despair.'

And so saying, the actress took her first steps into the pond. Unfortunately, where the grass met the water it had obviously become very slippery, and as her left foot began to slide a little away from her, she was forced to jerk herself backwards in order to regain her balance. And her dress, where it had become wet, rode up and clung damply to the sides of her leg. This revealed a quick glimpse of a pair of distinctly modern, high-heeled black boots.

Determinedly, she took a few more faltering steps into the water, but it was clear that the descent into the deceivingly benevolent-looking water was steeper than she'd anticipated. As she moved abruptly down, one arm shot out automatically in an attempt to keep her balance, and her reticule very neatly slipped off her arm and fell into the water with a heavy splash. Before she could snatch it back up again, it promptly sank from view into the muddy water.

Gamely Rachel ignored this slight faux pas, and whilst everyone else politely pretended not to notice it either, continued to walk gingerly into the pond. And Jenny, for one, didn't blame her. Although the watercourse had a pleasant, almost chocolate-box cosiness to it, it still must have felt distinctly odd and counterintuitive to take that first step into the cool water. Especially when so fully and elaborately dressed. And if she continued to look a little wobbly, and her movements were stiff and uncertain, who would be so churlish as to take notice? It couldn't have been easy to get this unrehearsed scene right first time, even for a seasoned actress.

And no matter what you might have thought of Rachel Norman the person, Rachel Norman the actress was clearly determined to do her audience proud. And Jenny for one silently took her hat off to her as she waded slowly but determinedly out towards the centre of the pond, where the little jetty cast a dark shadow over the glass-like water.

Feeling her way carefully with each step, she prepared to make the final, dramatic and fatal gesture of flinging herself face down into the water.

Everyone seemed to hold their breath as the water reached first her thighs and then her waist. Then, with a final loud and heartbroken sigh, she allowed herself to fall forward and become submerged, the silk of her dress ballooning out around her, her veil floating gently around her head and spreading out across the still water.

For the moment all was utterly silent as the appreciative audience took it all in, and then there was a collective sigh of released emotion at the stunning and genuinely moving sight of that body, floating gently on the water and beginning to drift lazily towards the wooden jetty.

Jenny, along with everyone else, instinctively raised her hands, getting ready to applaud.

And that was when all the screaming started.

* * *

Everyone, including Jenny, seemed to leap about six feet into the air. Her heart hammering sickeningly in her chest cavity, she whipped her head around instinctively, along with everyone else, in order to try and find the source of that awful sound.

The voice was female and clearly terrified. High-pitched with panic, it set the hairs on Jenny's neck standing on end, and she was not at all surprised to hear a little girl, who had to be about six or seven years old, start to cry in panic and shock. There was something hideously horrified and utterly uncontrolled in the ululating screams that split the air — something that spoke of nightmares and uncontrollable hysteria.

And because everyone was shifting about, trying to find the cause of the problem, a babble of voices asking 'what's up' and 'who is it' and 'bloody hell' filling the air, it took Jenny a moment to locate the cause of all the blood-curdling screaming.

And then her blue-eyed gaze quickly spotted Min Buckey, who seemed, ludicrously, to be doing some sort of a weird jig. She was bouncing around, her arms flailing wildly, as if trying to learn a particularly lively routine of the Highland Fling. It would almost have been comical if it wasn't for the look on her face.

She was sheet-white, her eyes enormous, her rather large mouth gaping open in a hideous and unattractive 'O.' Everyone was rushing towards her, wanting to help, but then drawing up short, since no one could see exactly what the problem was.

Beside her, her husband seemed to batting at something on her shoulder, whilst at the same time trying to talk her down. That she was deaf to his blandishments was obvious.

'Get it off . . . Oh, S-S-Si, get it off me! NOOOOOW!'

'Is she all right?' a tall, white-haired man said in the crowd, rather uselessly, since she clearly wasn't.

'It's OK, sweetheart, hold still,' Silas said loudly, trying to be heard over her screeching, whilst at the same time trying to catch his wife's flailing arms and keep her still. 'I can't see it — I'm sure it's dropped off. Honey, listen, I can't see it . . .'

Abruptly, Min Buckey sat down on the grass, for all the world like a puppet that had suddenly had all its strings cut. Those closest to her backed away, as if fearing that whatever she had might be catching. Quickly, and looking more and more frantic, her husband knelt beside her, still batting away at her clothes and imploring her to 'just breathe, honey, take some nice slow deep breaths. It'll be all right.'

And finally it began to dawn on Jenny just what the problem was, and she felt her shoulders, which had been excruciatingly tight with tension, begin to slowly relax.

'Min, honey, it's gone. I swear, I can't see it anywhere,' her husband said again.

'Oh, Si . . . oh, h-h-honey,' the poor woman began to sob helplessly. 'Oh, Si, get me away. I feel such a fool . . . all these people . . . Oh my, do I need a s-s-stiff drink. And then a lie down.'

There was a murmur of sympathy at this, as the American millionaire, without much ceremony, flexed his considerable bulk and hoisted his wife precipitously to her feet, where she stood swaying a little and looking rather dazed.

'What's the problem, mate?' some younger man in the watching crowd asked curiously, and Si waved a quick hand.

'Spider,' he said flatly. 'Nothing to worry about, and sorry for the fuss. My wife's terrified of 'em. We get some really nasty poisonous ones in the States, and one of her relatives died after being bitten. Ever since then, they terrify her.'

'Not surprised,' someone close to Jenny's right ear muttered sympathetically.

But overall, the words had the effect of making most people smile. And a definite ripple of relief spread throughout the crowd, gathering in momentum as the tension abruptly dissipated. The world was not coming to an end after all. There was no danger. Everything was fine. It was just a spider.

A slightly shamefaced Silas, and a still pale-as-a-sheet Min left the pond and began to walk falteringly away. And the crowd, now that the impromptu and unexpected show had come to an end, suddenly, and almost as one body, realised that they had, in fact, been in the middle of watching another performance, and everyone turned back to look at the pond.

Jenny fully expected to find Rachel Norman standing there fuming and mad as a wet cat at having her big moment upstaged so roundly.

Instead, her body was still gently floating face down by the little jetty.

It gave the cook a distinctly nasty start to see it there. Then, after considering it more rationally for a few seconds, she thought it made sense. For surely the actress, determined not to be outdone, must have seen what had happened and had waited in the pond until the attention began to turn back to her, and had then resumed her 'dead man's float' position.

With a wry smile, Jenny had to admire her perseverance and determination to see the scene through to the bitter end, and then reap the reward of her applause.

Impatient now to get it over with, Jenny began to clap. The others, most of whom had looked as surprised as Jenny to see the scene so unchanged, quickly followed her lead and also began to applaud.

A few people on the outer fringes, realising it was all over, began to turn and walk away, not even bothering to wait and watch the actress emerge in triumph from the pond.

The floating body didn't move.

Jenny frowned. Oh come on, Rachel, don't milk it, she silently urged her with a sigh.

The muted applause lessened.

But still the floating body didn't move.

And Jenny felt a cold shiver run up her spine. What was wrong with the wretched girl? Why didn't she just take her bow? OK, she might be feeling miffed at having her big moment ruined, but surely she . . .

Jenny stopped clapping. Surely Rachel must have heard them applauding her? Even if some part of her ears *were* underwater. So why wasn't she responding to her cue, eager to bask in her moment of glory?

Slowly, and as if Jenny's unease had communicated itself to the others, everyone fell ominously silent.

And still the gently floating body didn't move.

'Is she all right?' the white-haired man said again, and Jenny felt a weird sense of déjà vu.

Everyone seemed to take a tiny step closer to the edge of the pond, but no further. It was as if they were all paralysed and unable to do more than watch.

In the end it was Ion Dryfuss who gave a sudden savage oath, pushed his way through the crowd and launched himself unceremoniously into the water.

Still in numb, disbelieving silence, they all watched him wade frantically out towards her and grasp the floating arm nearest to him, pulling Rachel towards him. Once he'd got a better hold of her, he turned her over by her shoulders, thrusting the clinging wet veil that covered her face to one side.

And there was a sharp, collective moan. For the actress's eyes were wide open, and staring unseeingly at the sky. And any lingering hope on the part of the watching people that this might still be a part of the performance abruptly drained away.

And again Jenny could hear children start to cry, and wasn't surprised when their parents ushered them urgently away from the awful sight.

'Quickly, fetch her out! I know CPR,' called a thirty-something woman, dressed in jeans and a T-shirt advertising the wares of a local farmer's market. She pushed her way authoritatively to the front, galvanising the crowd to make way for her.

Almost sobbing with panic, the Welshman towed Rachel the short distance to the sloping edge of the pond, where several willing hands reached down to help him pull her up and onto the grass.

Everyone then fell back to give the woman room to work, except for Ion, who had fallen to his knees by Rachel's side and simply waited, staring mutely at his one-time lover's sodden, still beautiful, face.

Jenny heard several people around her reach for their mobile phones and call for an ambulance.

And Jenny knew that the police would be coming not far behind.

And what was already a nightmarish situation would soon become even worse.

CHAPTER SIX

People began to drift away, which worried Jenny slightly. She was pretty sure that the police were going to want to know who was present and take their statements. What's more, she'd noticed that a lot of the audience had been recording the scene on their mobile phones, and she was sure that the police would want to have copies of any footage.

Then she caught herself. Why was she assuming that the police would be so rigorous about all this anyway? This was surely either an accidental drowning, or maybe death by natural causes, wasn't it? Although she couldn't quite see how Rachel Norman might have accidentally drowned. Even if she hadn't been a strong swimmer, the pond was relatively small and the bank was almost within touching distance of the body. Besides, Jenny doubted that the pond could possibly be *that* deep, even in the very middle. Although Rachel was face down in the water, so she guessed that wouldn't even factor in. But how could she have accidentally drowned?

Unless she'd somehow become fatally entangled with the lime-green river weed, which had somehow managed to drag her down and kept her head submerged?

Thoughtfully, Jenny moved a little away from the small knot of people still helplessly shocked and clustered around the actress's lifeless body, and turned her attention to the pond itself.

For a few moments she studied it minutely. She could see the actress's footprints quite clearly where she'd gone in, the small, square cut of the modern high-heeled boots sinking in deeply in a distinctive pattern.

And no others.

So, clearly no one else had gone in after her when everyone was crowded around Min and had somehow managed to swim out to her and drown her, unobserved. Even Ion, who'd been the one to get her out, had all but taken a running jump from the grass, landing solidly out a couple of feet into the water.

The undeniably pretty river weed swayed innocently just underneath the water and looked harmless enough, and didn't seem to be particularly dense. In places, Jenny could clearly see the dark water underneath it. Surely there was not enough of it to become a real hazard?

Jenny sighed, feeling frustrated. Shock was clouding her thinking and she was beginning to doubt her ability to think logically. For surely even if Rachel *had* got into difficulties of any description, someone would have noticed and helped her out? Even with everyone crowding around the screaming and panicking Min, if the actress had been splashing about and gurgling, *someone* would have noticed. Those individuals who'd been at the back of the circle that had crowded around the hyperventilating American woman wouldn't have been able to see much of what was going on, and so would have been easily distracted by a splashing commotion going on behind them. Especially if Rachel had been calling for help.

No. Jenny gave a small shake of her head. It couldn't have happened that way.

Which only left natural causes.

Had the beautiful young girl had a heart attack or a stroke whilst in the water, and simply stopped breathing? Or a vicious cramp or some other paralysing spasm, or something which struck her suddenly and completely, leaving her dead in seconds, giving her no time to cry out for help?

Jenny, along with everyone else, had heard or read about the sad and frightening stories of how very fit and healthy young people could sometimes just up and die, right out of the blue. Some had been known to run marathons, or teach keep-fit, or do yoga instruction. On the face of it, they seemed the epitome of health and vitality. But, whilst making a cup of tea, or feeding the dog, they fell prey to a blood clot or coronary and were gone in moments, leaving behind stricken relatives or partners to cope with the incomprehensible loss.

So she knew it could happen.

Especially if Rachel had been one of those really unlucky people who had, all unknowingly, been suffering from some kind of undiagnosed weak heart or brain tumour. Perhaps the mild shock of the cool water, or the stress of doing her big scene, had served to exacerbate such a medical condition?

That made sense, in a sad kind of way.

So why was she so instinctively sure that that wasn't what had just happened here? Was she really so jaded or cynical that she instantly suspected foul play?

Feeling a little bit angry with herself, Jenny turned away from her contemplation of the pond, her eyes drifting restlessly around the rapidly diminishing crowd. And sighed slightly. The exodus wasn't *her* problem after all, and she certainly had no authority to tell them all that they should stay. And presumably the police would be able to ascertain just who had been here anyway, should it prove necessary. The village wasn't *that* big, and most people would be able to vouch for the presence of others. And there would be a list, somewhere, of all the historical society members, for sure. And as for the weekend guests who'd been staying at the inn, Jenny could vouch for them, since of them all only Dr Gilchrist had been absent, choosing, for whatever reason, to miss the highlight of the Regency Extravaganza. But then, he'd already admitted that the theatrics weren't really his cup of tea.

And neither of Rachel's fellow actors from the drama society had been here either, with Vince and Matthew presumably having better things to do. And then she brought herself up short. No, she had to make sure to be accurate now. To think and reason precisely.

She hadn't *seen* them here — but then she hadn't been looking out for them especially. That didn't mean to say that they weren't here. And, what with the villagers and other curious onlookers that they'd attracted on the walk to the pond adding to the number of the audience, there had been quite a crowd. It was perfectly possible that they'd been here amongst them and she hadn't seen them.

With a sigh, Jenny reminded herself, yet again, that it couldn't possibly matter. All of this speculation was just so much semantics. It would only matter who had alibis — and could prove them — if it turned out to be a case of murder.

And how could it possibly be murder?

Jenny's eyes refused to go to the sodden body lying on the grass. Instead her gaze shifted restlessly to those still grouped around her.

The woman who had bravely given CPR had now given up her ministrations and was sitting back on her heels, looking pale and miserable and defeated and close to tears. Jenny suspected she was probably going into mild shock. It was one thing to do your civic duty and be responsible and all that, and learn how to administer CPR, knowing that the chances had to be pretty good that you'd never be called upon to put it all into practice. But it was quite another thing to have to actually do something like that. And come face to face with a death that you hadn't been able to prevent. No wonder the poor woman was white-faced and shaky.

Some little way away from her, sitting blank-eyed and mute on the grass and staring straight out in front of him, Ion Dryfuss looked incapable of moving. It gave Jenny the spine-tingling feeling that Rachel's death had somehow drained him of all human thought and emotion, leaving him curiously aloof from everything around him.

Jenny's eyes rested on him thoughtfully.

Ion — the man who'd had a holiday romance with Rachel, and had then stubbornly followed her back to her home town, refusing to believe the affair was over. Clearly he'd been intent on trying to win her back, and had been openly unwilling to abide by the unspoken but cardinal rule: that holiday flings stayed at the resort.

Or was there another reason that he'd followed her back to the Cotswolds?

Perhaps, in thinking the best of him, Jenny had allowed her romantic nature to get the better of her. Because from what the travelling cook had been able to observe with her own eyes since becoming embroiled with the am-dram players, Rachel Norman had been, to say the least, rather cavalier, if not downright heartless, when it came to her relationships with men.

She had broken up her fellow actor Matthew Greenslade's engagement without any obvious signs of regret, or even any real understanding of the devastation she might have caused. And whilst Jenny might secretly think that Matthew's ex-fiancée had probably had a lucky escape, that wasn't really the point.

The point was, if Rachel could be so heartless and off-hand with one lover, she could be the same with another.

Perhaps her break-up with the Welshman had been similarly traumatic? Jenny could well believe that she might not have been very diplomatic about their break-up. What if Ion had begged her to stay and she'd just laughed in his face? Or had simply told him that a man from the Welsh valleys was hardly the kind of man she was looking for to help her fulfil her ambitions to become a famous actress?

Perhaps he had come here not for reconciliation but for revenge?

And thinking of Matthew's ex-fiancée, Jenny's mind raced on, perhaps *she* had been in the crowd, angrily watching Rachel's performance and becoming more and more aggrieved? Jenny certainly wouldn't know her from Adam (or Eve), and if she wasn't a resident of the village then neither, presumably, would anyone else.

Perhaps she hadn't taken the poaching of her man sitting down? Perhaps she . . .

And here, once again, Jenny brought herself to task. For what could the unknown fiancée, or anyone else with a grudge against the actress, have possibly done?

Waded into the pond, perhaps getting in at the back end behind the concealing curtain of weeping willows, and proceeded to drown Rachel in the few minutes whilst everyone was distracted by Min's screaming fit of arachnophobia? Hardly! She didn't care how bizarre Min's behaviour had been, or how intently everyone's attention had been focused on her, Jenny didn't believe that a crowd of thirty or more people could all have overlooked a young woman being drowned not six feet away from their noses.

It simply wasn't feasible.

And Rachel herself would hardly have allowed herself to be dragged under and drowned without screaming her head off or thrashing about like a mad thing.

Unless she'd been drugged first . . .

No. Stop it, Jenny told herself firmly. Now she really was wandering off into the realms of fantasy. She'd be concocting conspiracy theories next!

Rachel had walked from the Spindlewood Inn to the pond without once faltering or showing signs of being drugged or even feeling under the weather. And, what's more, she had delivered her lines in that wonderful, strong, sexy deep voice of hers without any hesitation or any slurring of her words.

And whilst Jenny might not be a chemist or medical professional, she couldn't think of any drug that could be administered and leave a patient clear-headed for a guaranteed amount of time before beginning to act. And one, moreover, that would then reliably render them unconscious or woozy and compliant enough — say twenty minutes later — in order for someone to then be able to drown them without them causing even a minor stir.

No. It was patently ludicrous. Even so-called date-rape drugs, which left a victim with no clear memory of events the next day, must surely affect them to such an extent that it would be noticeable to others? But Jenny, thinking back over the actress's performance, could see no evidence that she had been anything other than clear-headed at all times. Besides, how could anyone have predicted the scene caused by Min in which to plan such a thing?

So. Back to square one. It had to be either an accidental drowning or natural causes, Jenny told herself again. And trying to keep that thought firmly lodged in her mind, she turned away slightly, her eyes nevertheless skimming the edge of the pond. And saw something dark — very dark, lying just in the reeds near to where the actress had gone in.

In fact, not just dark, but actually black. Not large, but made of material that looked sodden and slightly muddy.

And suddenly, Jenny realised what it was she was looking at. Walking towards it, but careful not to touch it or disturb it in any way, Jenny crouched down to get a better look.

Yes. As she'd thought, it was the reticule — the pretty black beaded bag Rachel had been holding on to at the beginning of her big scene. Jenny squinted at it thoughtfully. It seemed to have a rather large hole in it at the bottom, presumably where the stitching had come away from the seams.

Looking at it, Jenny felt herself frowning.

But surely . . .

Just then, everyone heard the sound of sirens, insistent and shockingly loud and definitely getting closer, and Jenny's wandering thoughts screeched to a halt. Getting up from the edge of the pond and feeling, for some reason, oddly guilty, she turned her head and saw an ambulance making its way towards them down the narrow lane that led to the village green and pond.

And right behind it, the first of two police cars.

And here we go again, the travelling cook thought miserably.

In her various forays as a travelling cook, she'd had the misfortune to be present at a number of murders in the past couple of years, and she was getting all too familiar with police procedure. And how a murder case could turn lives upside down, with the innocent, along with the guilty, sometimes being devastated by the revelations that such a thorough and painstaking investigation could throw up.

Then there was the uncomfortable way that you gradually became suspicious of everyone around you, wondering if they could possibly be the killer. Along with the uneasy feeling that you were being watched all the time, and the slow, creeping sense of horror as you realised that there was a killer at loose somewhere nearby. And that you might be next!

All in all, Jenny Starling thought unhappily, I could do without this rigmarole again. Because no matter what her common sense told her, she was still convinced that someone, somehow, had contrived to very cleverly murder Rachel Norman. And as much as she'd like to think that she was just being unreasonably pessimistic, she was already beginning to compose her own testimony in her head.

But what, really, had she seen or heard that could possibly help the police?

* * *

DI Thomas Franklyn yawned slightly as his sergeant, Lucy O'Connor, indicated left and turned off from the main street and down a much narrower lane. Here garden walls festooned with purple flowers crowded either side of them, and swallows, getting ready to fly back to Africa, swooped and called in the clear blue sky.

'Pretty place, sir,' Lucy commented pleasantly. 'Though I bet it gets a bit too touristy in the high season.'

She was an attractive girl who was not looking forward to her thirtieth birthday next year, feeling that the landmark date had, rather unfairly, crept up on her unawares. She had large brown eyes and long blonde hair that she kept off her face in a no-nonsense ponytail. Her mother was constantly nagging at her to quit the force and settle down and produce children.

Previously she'd always tended to scoff at this, insisting that there would be plenty of time for all that later. But with the dreaded big three-oh birthday coming up, she was becoming more and more aware that 'later' might be looming closer than she would like.

However, since she was currently not even in a steady relationship, her mother would remain disappointed about potential grandchildren for some time to come.

Besides, right now Lucy had her eyes firmly on an inspector's position, and working with DI Franklyn could only help her achieve that goal. At forty-two, her superior officer was a good man to work for. Experienced, and with no hidden angst when it came to women in the workplace, he had a good, if rather pedestrian, track record when it came to closing his cases. But even better, he was known to be willing and able to pass on his knowledge and experience to those who wanted to learn.

Lucy felt herself lucky to be his bagman.

'Not for me, I'm afraid,' he said now in response to her observation, looking around him. 'Too twee and unreal for my liking. I feel like I'm walking onto the set of one of those Miss Marple things on telly. All chocolate-box and no reality.'

Thomas Franklyn had thinning black hair, eyes almost as black, and a neatly trimmed moustache that segued into a goatee beard. Married, divorced, married and divorced again, he now lived alone in a neat block of flats in Cheltenham, which his two grown sons from his first marriage tended to use as a flophouse when not attending university.

'It's a drowning, right?' he said now as his sergeant pulled the car to the side of the road, and they sat contemplating the milling scene in front of them.

Two patrol vehicles were parked either side of the lane, all but blocking it to passing traffic — not that there seemed to be a lot of that. Off to one side, a small group of people were clustered around a spot on the grass. Beyond them, a pleasant village pond, complete with reeds, weeping willows, pink-flowering bindweed and other assorted wildflowers, presented a suitably bucolic scene.

At least there weren't any ducks quacking about to get under his feet.

Lucy, looking around her at the bright summer's day, thought she understood what her boss meant about it all looking too picture-perfect. There were even butterflies and dragonflies darting around, looking as if they were waiting for a BBC wildlife documentary team to appear and start filming them.

'Well, best get on with it then,' the DI said a shade wearily, opening the passenger-side door and stepping out into the mellow afternoon.

It had been his sheer bad luck to be on call this Sunday. Even worse bad luck to be landed with a 'suspicious death' call. Not that he was expecting this death to be all that suspicious. Any unexplained death was noted down that way in the paperwork until it could be investigated and reclassified. And contrary to what all the crime shows on telly would have you believe, along with all those hundreds and hundreds of crime novels that filled the bookshops nowadays, by far and away most suspicious deaths turned out to be either natural causes or accidental. With a smattering of suicides thrown in for good measure.

Thankfully, murder was still a relatively rare occurrence, and Thomas had only ever worked on two cases of murder in his entire career. Which, in his opinion, was a fact to be grateful for. Give him the usual diet of burglaries, fraud, robbery, drunken affray and people trafficking any day.

If he'd wanted to specialise in murder he'd have joined the Met. Or asked for a transfer to any of the other major cities. But having been born and bred within sight of Cheltenham racecourse, he'd been quite content to stay in the Cotswolds.

Now, as he approached the little group in front of the absurdly placid and pretty pond, he noticed the bent head of Dr Martin Pryce, and some of his previous sangfroid evaporated.

There were several medical officers the police service used in the course of their callouts, but of them all Pryce was by far the most senior and experienced man. He'd worked in various hospitals and institutes of forensic pathology in his career, and was widely published in this sphere. What's more, in his time he'd even testified as an expert witness in quite a few high-profile murder cases, where independent expert testimony had been required, either by the defence or the prosecution.

It was only because the medico had left London a few years ago to semi-retire to a more rural and pretty spot that they had been able to engage his services at all. In his late forties, with a short cap of iron-grey curly hair, he had bright blue eyes and a rather sardonic sense of humour.

And it had probably been him who'd asked for an SIO of some rank to be called out. Which meant he wasn't happy about something.

Now the medical man looked up as he watched them approach, his eyes going first — and appreciatively — to Lucy, before sliding across to Franklyn. Quickly, the DI hid a smile and firmly resisted the impulse to smirk.

He'd heard it bandied about on the grapevine that the doctor had an eye for the ladies — which was something that his long-suffering wife (according to the same grapevine) had long since learned to put up with. And now he rather thought that the grapevine had it right — for once.

'DI . . . Franklyn, isn't it?' Dr Pryce said curtly, rising to his feet. Not a particularly tall man, he nevertheless moved with an energy that seemed irrepressible, making him appear somehow bigger. 'And this is . . . ?' he fished shamelessly, holding out his hand and smiling, his penetrating blue eyes fixed firmly on Thomas's sergeant.

Franklyn was a little irritated to note that Lucy was blushing slightly, and was clearly not averse to being the centre of the doctor's attention.

'Sergeant O'Connor. I take it this is an accidental drowning?' he said tersely, for the first time paying proper attention to the corpse at his feet. And the first thing that surprised him, taking him utterly aback, was the fact that she was wearing a long black dress. And was that a veil over her face? What the hell? He blinked, then realised that she was just a follower of gothic fashion. Obviously their victim had been one of those women who liked to go about looking like they belonged in a horror film.

And had Rachel been in any condition to know that she'd been so overlooked until now, especially when she might reasonably have expected to be the centre of attention, the actress would have been seriously put out, Jenny mused as she watched everything closely.

Then she felt slightly sick that she could think something so flippant at a time like this. The poor girl was dead. Jenny sighed heavily, knowing that her thoughts were all over the place because she was still in shock and felt so unsettled.

'I'm not so sure about that,' Dr Pryce answered the DI's question quietly — too quietly for any of the nearest bystanders to hear. He indicated the body, and once more crouched down on his knees beside her.

Franklyn, brought up short by the doctor's unexpected answer, also squatted down, careful to keep the knees of his trousers from actually touching the damp ground.

'There's no frothing in the mouth for a start,' Martin Pryce said, 'which I would have expected, had the victim inhaled water.' And he then proceeded to give the inspector a rather complicated but mercifully short lecture on various other signs and indications that should have been present at a drowning — and weren't.

He then pointed out various other anomalies so rapidly that, at the end of it all, Franklyn wasn't much clearer than when the medical man had begun.

'So, you think . . . what, exactly?' he asked flatly. Unlike many other SIOs, Franklyn had never felt the need to come across as if he knew everything about everything, and had never had any concerns about asking straightforward questions. In his view, it often saved a lot of time and confusion. If you didn't know something — just ask. Some smug bugger was usually more than happy to enlighten you.

'I'm not sure,' Dr Pryce said cautiously. 'And until I've had her on my table and been given the chance to have a good rootle about, I won't *be* sure either. And I want to get started on that right away.' He glanced at his watch. 'Might as well — my Sunday's ruined anyway. Oh, and I'll need to do a diatom test of course, just to be sure, as well as getting some other blood work done. Just in case we are talking natural causes here.'

Franklyn frowned slightly. He knew a little something about diatoms — they were some kind of microscopic organisms found in water; a species of algae, presumably. So if you detected their presence in the lungs of drowning victims, you could compare it to a water sample taken at the scene, thus confirming that the victim had indeed inhaled water from the same place that they were found. Or not, as the case might be, in which case you knew that the body had been moved after death.

'You're sounding more and more as if you suspect foul play,' he complained, getting to his feet and pretending not to hear his knees click ominously as he did so.

'Let's just say,' Dr Pryce said, also rising to his feet but with considerably less noise, 'that I wouldn't be so eager to sign off on this as an accidental drowning just yet. Not that I'm saying it might not turn out to be the case after all, mind!'

Which, in Franklyn's experience, was typical of medical men. 'Right. OK. Well then, in that case,' he grumbled, 'O'Connor,' he turned to his sergeant, 'we'd better call out the works. I want photographs and a fingertip search of the immediate area organised. Better tell the uniforms the good news. Oh, and get a diver in to do a sweep of the pond. I dare say he won't find anything except the usual obligatory shopping trolley, but it had better be done.'

'Yes, sir,' Lucy said smartly. 'I know someone on the diving team; he lives quite close by. He loves getting wet, sir, so I don't think he'll mind coming out on a Sunday. I also think that he and his diving buddy will probably be able to cover this little pond on their own,' she advised. It didn't hurt to give her boss a gentle reminder that their superintendent wouldn't be too pleased with paying overtime, let alone stretching the budget to cover the use of the whole diving team.

'Oh. Yes, right,' Franklyn agreed vaguely. Like most men tasked with actually solving crimes, he tried not to worry about such things.

He took a quick look around at the small group of people who were still milling around on the periphery and watching him curiously, but his eyes quickly settled on the wet and shivering young man who was standing a little away from the others. Leaning against a low stone wall, he was looking morosely down at his feet.

This, presumably, had been the one who had gone in the water and dragged the body from the pond. Had he been first on the scene? Clearly, interviewing him was a priority.

His eyes moved further on, went past a tall, rather striking-looking woman with long dark hair and dazzling blue eyes, on to another woman who looked rather pale and shaken . . . And then, stiffening slightly, his eyes jerked back to the tall, dark-haired woman.

'I know her,' he blurted out loud.

But since Lucy had, by now, already moved away to make the phone call to her diving friend and organise the uniforms into cordoning off the area and starting a search, he was speaking only to himself.

Instantly, the policeman's mind went into overdrive. First he racked his brains for known criminals. But no female perpetrators matched this woman's description. Was she some local celebrity? Had he seen her on some local news station? No. It was definitely something related to police work. Something that was making him feel rather uneasy. Something . . .

And then he remembered.

'Oh bloody hell,' he muttered.

And Jenny Starling could only watch, appalled, as what was clearly the police officer in charge of the scene made an uncompromising beeline straight for her.

She felt her spine stiffen instinctively as he approached. She had been hoping that, this time around, she could slip under the radar and go unnoticed.

'It's Miss Starling, isn't it?' DI Franklyn said flatly, the moment he was in range of her. And the people who'd been standing either side of her instantly moved nervously away, like a flock of sheep suddenly spotting a predator in their midst, or as if she might somehow have become contagious. And all of them were clearly wondering why she'd been singled out for such instant attention.

Feeling a bit like a leper, Jenny heaved a sigh.

'Yes,' she acknowledged simply.

Thomas Franklyn nodded glumly. 'I thought so.'

First of all, Dr Martin Pryce wasn't happy about cause of death. And now there was this woman on the scene. Although he wasn't a superstitious man, he wryly acknowledged to himself that the omens could hardly be more ominous if a group of crows were perched on a wall glaring down at him.

For Franklyn knew all about the travelling cook. Most coppers in the area did.

'So, I suppose you already know who did it and can give me the name of the guilty party on a plate?' he asked, irony and sarcasm vying for first place in his tone.

Jenny blinked, a little taken aback by the forthright attack.

'Sorry?' she temporised.

Franklyn sighed. 'Miss Starling, I'm well aware that, in the past, let's just say that you've proven to be a very useful *witness*,' he stressed the word tellingly. 'This isn't the first time you've been present when someone has died, not by a long shot. So don't come with the all-innocent act, OK?'

Jenny bowed her head in silent acknowledgement.

'So shortly I'm going to ask you to give me a competent and reliable statement about what you know about this,' he waved a hand at the black-clad body on the grass.

He watched her carefully, trying to dredge up from his memory what several of his fellow police officers had said about her, when they'd had the misfortune to lead a murder investigation where this woman had been present.

Hadn't all of them told him that she could be both immensely helpful, and at the same time utterly annoying?

'She misses nothing, and has a clear and logical mind,' Franklyn could now remember one of them saying. 'If you ever come across her, keep an eye on her, or else she'll make a total fool of you,' he'd then gone on to warn him.

And so, bearing that in mind, he reached out a hand to take her arm, intending to lead her to a quiet little corner and ask just how she came to be here, and what the hell was going on.

But before he could do so, however, a young uniformed officer came rushing up to him. He sounded slightly breathless with excitement, his eyes all but gleaming with glee. Clearly, this was his first major case, and he was feeling jubilant.

'Sir, sir, you need to see this,' he said urgently. 'We've found a firearm!'

CHAPTER SEVEN

'What?' Franklyn yelped, his jaw dropping open, looking and sounding actually gobsmacked. 'You found a *gun*? What kind of gun?'

His mind raced. Surely the victim couldn't have been shot, was his very first thought. For one thing it was impossible for him to believe that the legendary Dr Pryce might have missed something so obvious as a gunshot wound — in fact, his mind practically boggled at the very idea. Even given the fact that the corpse was dripping wet and concealed head to toe in that outlandish black garment, which might make spotting even a rather large bloodstain very difficult, it was hard to believe such an oversight had happened.

Beside him, Jenny Starling too was staring at the uniformed PC in astonishment, her mind feverishly going over the events of the past hour or so. Although she had no idea of the attending physician's almost legendary status in the local CID, she *was* concerned with her own powers of observation — or maybe lack thereof.

Surely she would have heard and recognised a gunshot if she'd heard one? Even if, somehow, the killer had managed to fire a round at the peak of one of Min's frantic screams, a shot would echo louder than a human voice, surely? And especially at such close range. Unless they'd used a silencer, maybe?

But immediately as she thought it, she felt stupid. Silencers on guns were something you saw in those slick American thrillers on television or at the cinema. But not in real life, surely? And most definitely not in a sleepy little Cotswold village, for Pete's sake! The area was hardly known for being a hotspot for gangsters!

'It's an air rifle, sir,' the PC admitted at once, and a little less enthusiastically now, trying not to notice the way his superior's shoulders slumped in relief, or the way his brow was starting to furrow with annoyance at the way he'd delivered the news so dramatically. 'It's just lying in the long grass, over there,' he swept on quickly, and pointed to a spot on the far side of the pond, where his colleague was waiting, obviously guarding their find.

Franklyn, letting out his breath in a relieved gush, ran a harassed hand through his already thinning hair. When he'd first heard the word 'firearm' he'd instantly thought of a handgun, and thus had been utterly perplexed. Why would there be a gun at the scene? Now, he supposed, it made a bit more sense. 'I dare say some yokel just left it there when he was out shooting crows or pigeons or something,' he muttered angrily.

But even as he offered this explanation to the now slightly red-faced constable, he could feel his brow furrow in a frown. Because why *would* a local leave his air rifle behind? It was a reasonably expensive item after all, and wasn't the sort of weapon you could easily forget about, was it? It was a weighty, long and rather inconvenient thing to have about you. Was it really something that you could just put down for whatever reason and then wander off, forgetting that you'd brought it out with you when you left the house? Hardly! And why put it down on the ground at all?

Jenny Starling was wondering the exact same thing. Just like Franklyn, she was staring over at the spot where the weapon had been found. Although she'd never used one herself, her grandfather had, and her memory of it had been of a wooden-handled rifle with a long metal barrel. A fairly heavy and sturdy piece of kit, it had fascinated her, simply because it had been a gun. What's more, the only gun, as far as she knew, that ordinary members of the public of his generation had a right to use with impunity. For that reason alone, she'd been drawn to it. But she hadn't thought about it in years, and now she racked her brain for more up-to-date information.

Did you have to have a licence for them nowadays, she wondered, and thought it highly likely that you did, given the modern-day obsession with such things. Gone were the days when you could just casually have these things and think nothing of it. And yet, having said that, in a rural community like this, there probably *were* still dozens of the things to be found, lying forgotten or unregistered in attics or outhouses.

If her memory served her right, they fired little single-shot round lead pellets or some such thing. But what on earth was it doing here though? As a potential murder weapon it seemed absurdly inadequate. It wasn't exactly the kind of weapon that could do anyone much damage, surely? Maybe take an eye out, if you were unlucky.

Impatiently, Jenny shook her head. There she went again — her mind instantly turning to thoughts of murder! It was a simple air rifle, not a sniper's rifle! And besides, Rachel had drowned, or had a heart attack. Either way, she certainly hadn't been shot — either with an air rifle or anything else.

'Well, you'd better show me I suppose,' Franklyn said with a distinct lack of enthusiasm. Then, turning to point an imperious finger at Jenny, added darkly, 'Please don't go anywhere, Miss Starling. I still want to have that word with you.'

Jenny blinked. 'Of course,' she said faintly.

And ignoring the curious look the PC gave her, she wandered over to a nearby wooden bench, set against a low-built stone wall, and sat down heavily. It felt good to take the weight off her feet. She was beginning to feel that this had been a very long day already, and it was not over yet, not by a long shot.

Further along the wall, she noticed that Ion was leaning, gently steaming in the warm summer air as his wet clothes began to dry out, and looking blankly down at his feet. He was wearing white trainers that were now sodden and stained slightly green where some algae from the pond had stuck to them. He still looked shell-shocked and disbelieving, and every now and then, a series of shivers would wrack his frame.

She had a vague idea that he'd been seen by the paramedics who had come in the ambulance, and the fact that he hadn't been whisked away to A&E reassured her somewhat that they hadn't deemed his condition serious enough to warrant further medical attention.

She wondered if she should go to him and try and offer some words of comfort. But then she acknowledged grimly that there was probably no comfort that she could possibly offer him that would be of use, and decided to leave the poor man alone with his grief.

* * *

Over by the far side of the pond, Franklyn stared down at the rifle, lying concealed in a thick patch of tall, rough couch grass. He frowned, wondering if this had been a deliberate attempt to hide it. Or had someone simply been out looking for rabbits or pigeons to pop into their pie, and had sat down in this pleasant spot near the pond for a rest? Maybe they'd even been tempted by the Indian summer heat to do a last bit of sunbathing. It wasn't much of a stretch to think that they might then have dozed off before rousing themselves and going home.

Forgetting all about the rifle? Granted it wasn't as significant as a shotgun. But even so . . . But perhaps an older person, getting a little bit senile? It certainly didn't look like a modern rifle — it had an old-fashioned hefty look to it. So that might fit. Some old codger who still liked to play the role of a mighty hunter.

He sighed heavily. Here was yet another complication he could do without. Chances were it had nothing at all to do with the matter in hand, but it would take up their valuable time and resources in checking it out. 'Better get it tagged up and printed,' he told the man guarding it. 'Then see if it has any serial numbers on it, anything that can help you trace who might have owned it. Oh, and get someone to take a photo of it and show it around the village. Hopefully someone will recognise it and come forward to claim it.' That is, if they had an innocent explanation for why it was here.

'Sir.' The elder of the PCs looked sceptical, as well he might. The rifle didn't look new to him either, and he'd already decided that the chances of successfully tracing it were likely to be very slim indeed. What's more, he thought the odds were very high that no villager, no matter how innocent they were, would not be all that keen to admit to owning it. Not once it got around that it was now the object of an official police investigation. In his experience, nobody liked to get mixed up in things that could end up with them having to testify in court. And this scenario would be only more likely if the owner hadn't ever bothered to get a proper licence for it.

In these hard financial times, having to pay a fine or spend precious hours off work sorting out a legal wrangle would be something any sane person would be keen to avoid. And if whoever owned the rifle *did* have something to do with the death of a young girl, then he'd be a fool to bring himself to the police's attention.

Franklyn nodded at them to get on with it, then tramped back towards the pond.

It was time he got the full picture from that Starling woman. Since it seemed it was his turn to be stuck with her, he might as well make use of her fabled sleuthing powers. And who knew — she might actually live up to her reputation and have something worthwhile to tell him.

On the way over, Lucy O'Connor waylaid him, and told him that the two-man diving team couldn't do a sweep of the pond until first thing tomorrow morning. Franklyn told her that was fine, and ploughed on.

If his sergeant was surprised by the set, rather grim look on his face as he left her, she showed no sign of it.

* * *

'So, I assume you were just taking an afternoon stroll and happened to see a body in the water?' he asked Jenny a few minutes later, sitting down heavily beside her on the bench.

At this unpromising and totally unexpected start, Jenny shot him a startled look. 'Oh no, Inspector . . . er . . .'

'Franklyn.'

'Franklyn. No, I wasn't just passing by at all. None of us were,' she added, waving a hand around at the people who'd stayed to watch what happened next. 'We'd all come to watch her drown, you see,' Jenny said helpfully.

Then she paused as the policeman's eyes almost bugged out, realised what she'd just said, and, with a sinking heart, concluded that so far nobody had had the chance to tell him the true circumstances surrounding the incident. 'Oh hell, I'd better start from the beginning,' she put in quickly.

'Yes, I rather think you'd better,' the inspector said grimly. 'What on earth do you mean, you all came to watch her drown? Was it a spectator sport or something?' he added viciously. Already he had the nasty suspicion that he wasn't going to like what she had to tell him, and he could feel a growing sense of grievance taking up residence in his stomach.

When he'd got the call to come out all he'd been told was that a woman had drowned in a village pond, and had been pulled out by a member of the public. Naturally, given that it was such a nice sunny Sunday afternoon, he'd expected to find that someone walking their mutt had noticed the floating body and called it in. And he'd assumed that the small crowd that he and his sergeant had found on arrival had simply been the usual collection of ghoulish onlookers that tended to gather around any tragic incident.

Nine times out of ten, that — or something similar — was what happened in cases such as this. But clearly this episode was going to be an exception to the rule, and Franklyn didn't like those. In his experience, exceptions to the rule had a habit of causing him a major headache.

And so Jenny spent the next ten minutes bringing him up to speed, trying to be as accurate and as inclusive as she could with her information, and filling him in on everything that had happened since her arrival at the Spindlewood Inn. In detail, she explained what the Regency Extravaganza weekend had entailed, along with a description of the am-dram performances, and the people she had met thus far.

She gave him a brief outline of all that she had learned about her employers, the Americans, the Oxford don, the Welshman and the actors. And, of course, Rachel Norman and her rather lackadaisical attitude to the men in her life.

Jenny wasn't really surprised to note that the policeman's already glum face became gradually gloomier and gloomier with every word she said.

When she'd finished, Franklyn sighed heavily. 'So this woman, Rachel Norman,' he swept a hand towards the body, 'is an actress. Come to think of it, I did wonder why she was in that get-up. Now it makes more sense — she was doing the final scene where her character drowns herself?'

'Yes.'

'And everyone watched her walk into the pond,' he persisted, wanting to be sure he now had a clear and comprehensive picture of what had occurred during the last hour or so.

'Yes.'

'And then this other woman, this American who's so scared of spiders, started screaming?'

'Yes.'

'And everyone fussed over her for a while.'

'Yes.'

Franklyn, who was scribbling frantically in his notebook, looked up. 'Can you say for how long this went on?

That you were all so distracted, I mean, and not looking at what was happening in the pond anymore?'

Jenny took a long, slow breath. She understood at once, of course, how important that question was. And so she was very careful about giving her answer. She needed to get this right.

'Well, it's rather hard to say,' she began apologetically. 'When something's happening in real time, and it's something shocking and unexpected, time often seems to pass faster than you think, doesn't it?'

Franklyn thought about this for a moment or two, and rather cautiously nodded agreement. 'Yes. And conversely, when you're bored, time seems to drag. OK, let's try and break it down a bit, and see if we can't arrive at something that has a chance of being accurate. Someone screams. You all turn and look. That must have been instinctive and instantaneous. You all see this woman dancing about, panic-stricken. Say . . . ten seconds? You watch her husband try and comfort her, you figure out what the problem is. There's been a spider on her. Say, another twenty to thirty seconds. She falls to the ground. Everyone's concerned and gathers around. Say, another ten to twenty seconds. Her husband takes charge and gets her to her feet and they move off. So, perhaps no more than a minute has passed?'

Jenny sighed. 'When you say it like that, it seems too short a time frame,' she eventually said. 'I think it was probably a bit longer than that.'

'Five minutes?' the policeman offered tentatively.

'Oh no,' Jenny said at once. 'I don't think it was as long as all that. Maybe two to three minutes? Four at the most — but I'd have said less. Three minutes, give or take, is the best I can do. Sorry,' she shrugged, feeling a bit of a fool. So much for her past experiences of murder leading her to being a so-called expert witness!

Franklyn heaved a sigh at this, but nodded. He was used to witnesses being all over the place, but her account had sounded reasonable enough.

'So after these Americans left — I presume they went back to this inn you're all staying at?' he put in sharply.

'The Spindlewood Inn, yes. It's situated on one side of the main village square,' Jenny said. 'At least, I *imagine* that's where they went.' Then she frowned. Was she, once again, in danger of giving misleading testimony? After all, she didn't know *for sure* that that was where they'd gone. She was simply assuming it. For all she knew, right now Min and Silas Buckey might be high-tailing it in a taxi for Heathrow airport. 'But I can't think that they'd have gone anywhere else, Inspector. I'm sure I remember Min saying that she needed a stiff drink, so it seems likely that's where they'd go. They'd hardly have gone anywhere else — they were both still dressed in their costumes, you see.'

Franklyn sighed. 'But most of the crowd were dressed normally,' he said, glancing up at the spectators. Although there were one or two people still dressed like something from a BBC drama, for the most part the crowd were dressed in light summer casuals.

'Yes. Only those participating in the Regency Extravaganza came in costume. Most of these people,' Jenny nodded around her, 'were onlookers that we sort of picked up on the way.'

Franklyn nodded, still scribbling her answers down in his notebook in what, to Jenny, looked like very neat and competent shorthand.

Mentally, he made a note that he needed to speak to these Buckey people as soon as possible. Because one thing at least, in this whole mess of a tale, was now becoming clear. If anything untoward *had* happened to Rachel Norman in that pond, then it was a mighty big coincidence that the American woman had created such a distraction just when it must have been needed the most.

'Did you get the feeling that this Buckey woman was faking it?' he asked her sharply.

Jenny instantly followed his logic, and sighed. So, it was starting again. Just as she'd known it would.

Always before, whenever she got mixed up in murder, she'd felt this similar burden of responsibility eventually weighing her down. Where every word she said was fraught with danger. What if she said something that brought an innocent person under suspicion? What if she forgot about a vital little piece of evidence, or misinterpreted something that let a guilty person walk free?

Already she could begin to feel the whole wearying cycle starting up again, and told herself to buck up. If Rachel's death had been deliberately planned, then she owed it to the dead girl to do all she could to help the police solve the case.

'OK, let me think,' she said reluctantly, casting her mind back to the first time that she'd heard the scream. It had sounded high-pitched and panic-stricken and it had raised the hairs on the back of her neck.

And when she'd first seen Min, her face had been contorted in fear and panic; her eyes were huge, her mouth gaped open, and she had been as white as milk. There had been nothing pretty or, in her opinion, fake, about the performance. But then, what did she really know about Min? For all she knew, she could have been an actress, just like Rachel, before meeting and marrying her rich husband.

'Let's just say if she was faking it then she was a far better actress than Rachel,' Jenny finally said, feeling that she'd given as honest an answer as was possible.

The policeman, who'd been watching her intently, grunted slightly. He knew himself to be as good a judge of character as anyone else, and he rather thought — despite her reputation as being a pain in the constabulary's arse — that Jenny Starling was a very clever, and honest, person.

Which had the effect of making him feel a little more kindly towards her. Perhaps he really should stop seeing her as another stumbling block to be overcome, and more of an asset.

'OK,' he said mildly, filing away her answer and moving on. 'So they go off and you all remember that you'd been watching this actress and her big suicide scene, and all turn back to look at her and see how the scene's progressing?' he prompted.

And for a moment, Franklyn hesitated, his own words echoing oddly in his head. *Her big suicide scene.*

He hadn't seriously been considering suicide up until now. But what if the woman had decided to commit suicide for real? For all they knew at this point, Rachel Norman might have had all sorts of problems in her life that would soon come to light. Love troubles. Debts maybe. She might even have had a terminal illness. And she was an actress, when all was said and done, with a thespian's sense of the dramatic. Dying for real in front of her audience might have appealed — especially if she wasn't quite right in the head, and wanted to go out in spectacular style.

But then, it had to be hard to actually make yourself drown, surely? He found himself frowning. Surely the instinct to gulp for air, even if you wanted to die, would prove to be all but . . . Damn it, no, that wouldn't work either. The reason Dr Pryce was so antsy was because he didn't think she *had* drowned.

'That's right,' Jenny Starling was saying now, dragging him back to the facts. 'And we noticed that she didn't seem to be moving. So we all started clapping and applauding, and expected her to get up and take a bow. But she didn't. She just kept right on floating there.' Jenny paused and sighed pensively. 'I think right there and then, we all realised at more or less the same moment that something was seriously wrong.'

'OK, slow down a bit,' Franklyn adjured her patiently. 'When you all turned from Min Buckey and looked at the pond, did you notice anything odd or out of place?'

Jenny blinked. 'Can you be a bit more specific, Inspector?' she asked cautiously.

Franklyn grunted, less patiently now, but obliged. 'Did anyone's behaviour strike you as odd, for instance?'

'No.'

'Did you think anyone was closer to the edge of the water than they should have been?'

'No.'

'Did you notice if anyone had wet clothes?'

'No.'

The inspector sighed. It had been a long shot — and he was becoming confident that if this woman had noticed anything helpful, she'd already have said so. Still, he had to ask.

'OK. So, it's at this point that the Welsh fellah jumps in and pulls her out?' he queried, casting a quick wave in Ion Dryfuss's direction. 'And you're sure, when he went in the water, that he wasn't already wet?'

'Yes. I'm sure I'd have noticed if he was already wet,' Jenny said confidently.

'Now, let's just make sure I've got this right. The chap that pulled her out, according to you, first met her when she went on holiday earlier this year, and followed her back here? And he's sweet on her you think?'

'Ye-es,' Jenny said, a little less certainly now. 'But that's just the impression I got, picking things up here and there. I might have it all wrong. You should really ask him about all that.'

Franklyn, for the first time, smiled a genuine smile. 'Thanks for the tip,' he said dryly. 'I might just do that in a bit.'

Jenny flushed faintly. 'Sorry, Inspector. Not trying to teach my grandma how to suck eggs or anything,' she apologised. 'I just don't want to be responsible for misleading you or saying something that later turns out to have a different explanation. You must bear in mind that I've only known all these people a matter of thirty-six hours or so. You can't really rely on me to get everything right. I can only tell you my version of events.'

The inspector felt oddly chastised and quickly shook his head. 'Yes, I understand that. And I'm grateful for your input. Really. You're being very helpful.'

Jenny shrugged off the compliment. 'Is there anything else I can tell you?'

There was plenty, and the inspector was keen to get to it. 'How long did it take him to get her to the shore?'

'Oh, seconds only. As you can see, it's not a very big expanse of water, is it?'

'And he managed to get her out and onto the grass on his own?'

'Oh no. I think several of the men who were on the edge of the bank reached down to help him pull her up once he'd got her to the edge — and sorry, before you ask, no, I don't think I can point them out,' Jenny said. Her head was beginning to feel as if it was full of cotton wool. That was another thing she was beginning to remember from her last close call with murder. Just how exhausting it all was. And realising just how much you failed to notice about what was actually going on around you.

It always left her feeling so inadequate!

'But I'm sure that, whoever they were, they'd have told your police officers about it by now,' she added.

Franklyn nodded. No doubt she was right — it was human nature to want to get kudos for playing the hero, no matter how humble the heroics had been.

'And this is when the woman who knew CPR took over.' Franklyn already had her name noted down, and would have to talk to her later.

'Yes. But it was clear that Rachel wasn't responding,' Jenny said quietly.

Franklyn glanced at her thoughtfully. 'From what you've told me, you didn't really like Miss Norman, did you?' he said. His voice was level, making it less of an accusation, and more like an offer to expand on a statement.

Jenny shrugged. 'Sorry. But I can't say as I thought she was a particularly likeable person. I know no one likes to speak ill of the dead . . . It seems so sneaky and unfair, doesn't it, when they can't defend themselves. But . . .' And again, she shrugged.

'I understand. But it's vital we know as much about her as possible,' the inspector insisted. 'And I trust your judgement.'

Jenny nodded. 'OK. I think she was ferociously ambitious. She seemed determined to make it to the big time as an actress. She was taking lessons, getting professionally photographed, courting the press . . . Generally, doing everything she could to get ahead. And ambitious people can be short-sighted and tactless.'

'So we'll probably find that she wasn't very popular with her fellow am-dram performers,' Franklyn put in wryly.

'Probably not. I've already told you that she enjoyed the company of men,' Jenny put in dryly. 'And she also seemed to like money.'

'Can you expand on that?'

Jenny shrugged. 'She always seemed to wear designer-label clothes, and expensive perfume and make-up. And she was probably on the lookout for a rich sugar daddy, if the play she made for Silas Buckey was anything to go by.'

Franklyn visibly brightened at this. The rich Americans again. Yes, he was definitely looking forward to speaking to them. 'Do you think they were sleeping together? The rich American guy and Rachel?'

Jenny shook her head. 'I really doubt it. It always seemed to me that Silas was rather fond of his wife.'

But then, she could be wrong. That was another thing Jenny had learned from her past experiences with murder. Anyone could be wrong about anything.

'All right. Well, I think that's it for the moment. But I'll probably want to talk to you again at some point.'

Jenny nodded glumly and without surprise. She fully expected to be answering questions for days to come. 'Fine,' she said wearily.

'It's all a bit of a mess isn't it?' he said sympathetically.

Jenny looked him squarely in the face. 'But surely Rachel must have had a heart attack or something, mustn't she?' she proffered hopefully. 'Nothing else really makes any sense, does it?'

But if she was hoping that Inspector Franklyn would confirm her hopes or negate her doubts, she was doomed to be disappointed. For he merely gave a distinctly non-committal grunt and left her, heading purposefully towards Ion.

She saw the man from the Welsh valleys glance up at his arrival, then go instantly back to staring down at his feet.

CHAPTER EIGHT

Jenny, not quite sure whether or not she'd been officially dismissed, and therefore now free to return to the inn, glanced around uncertainly.

During her long interview with the inspector, more police reinforcements had arrived, and she noticed that all the remaining spectators were busily giving their details to the uniformed officers, along with, she supposed, a brief description of what they'd all seen and heard. She noticed that many of them were also transferring photographs and videos that they'd made of the event from their mobile phones, onto the police officers' own devices. And she could only hope that they revealed something vital, because at that moment she hadn't got anything even remotely approaching a clue as to what could have happened that had resulted in Rachel Norman being killed.

A blue-and-white police tape cordon was in the process of being set up to keep people from trespassing around the circumference of the pond, and several other police officers were on their hands and knees doing a minute and painstaking search of the grass and bank surrounding it.

But most distressing of all, Rachel Norman's body was just being slipped discreetly and chillingly into a black body bag, in readiness to be taken away to the waiting coroner's mortuary van that had now taken the place of the unnecessary ambulance.

Hastily averting her gaze from this macabre scene, Jenny became distracted by a movement off to her left. And, turning her head, she saw a woman on the far side of the pond, near to the path that led to the little jetty that went out to the middle of the water. She seemed to be staring across at the scene, as if looking for something. Or, perhaps, someone.

But making their way steadily towards her were the police officers with the blue-and-white police tape and little metal poles, who were intent on securing the area. As Jenny watched, one officer would competently hammer a little metal pole into the grass, whilst the other one wound the tape around and through it, before looping it along to the next pole.

The woman suddenly seemed to notice their approach and quickly set off. But not towards Jenny and the others, where a path leading back to the village could be found, but instead setting off across the rough field beyond. Clearly, she didn't want to have to talk to the police, or be seen by any of the other spectators who were still hanging around.

Which instantly made Jenny sit up and take extra notice. So intent was she on watching this distinctly suspicious behaviour that it took a while for the cook to realise that she'd actually seen the woman somewhere before.

Jenny didn't know why, but she'd have been willing to bet money (well, a modest amount!) that the stranger wasn't just another random villager. Not someone who'd merely been lured out to see what was going on and, whilst curious to see what was happening, was at the same time anxious not to get actively involved.

What's more, even from the quick glimpse that she'd just had of her, Jenny was now sure that the woman making her way smartly across the open field was the same red-haired woman in the trouser suit who'd been sitting at the bar at the inn the other day. The woman that she'd then subsequently seen talking angrily with Dr Rory Gilchrist sometime later, before storming off in a huff.

Jenny had assumed that she was Rory Gilchrist's ex-wife, or an ex of some sort, and almost certainly the woman the Oxford academic had been so anxious to avoid that he'd actually paid to spend a weekend away from his home town.

Now what was *she* doing here, Jenny wondered. The cook hadn't formed the impression that she'd been part of the Regency Extravaganza. And she wasn't a guest at the inn, that was for sure.

What's more, Jenny pondered thoughtfully, if *she* was here, was Rory also somewhere nearby? Quickly, she glanced around her, but there was still no sign of the silver fox. But had the woman expected to find him here and come looking for him? If he was deliberately avoiding her — and after their argument of the other evening that was a good bet — perhaps she'd had trouble tracking him down and had hoped to confront him again here?

Telling herself that all this speculation was pointless — what she badly needed were some plain and simple *facts* to go on — Jenny got up and approached a nearby uniformed police officer who had just finished talking to one of the villagers.

'Hello. My name is Miss Jenny Starling. I've already spoken to Inspector Franklyn. I just wanted to make sure that I could go now?' she asked politely.

'Of course, madam. Can I just make sure I have your home address please? And contact details?'

Jenny gave him her mobile phone number and told him that she was currently staying at the Spindlewood Inn in the centre of the village. And when she heard him give her the go-ahead to leave, she felt a profound sense of relief. She just didn't want to be in this lovely little beauty spot anymore. In fact, if she never saw another village pond again, she wouldn't much care.

The short walk back to the inn felt a bit surreal. It was now nearly six in the evening, and the sun was beginning to sink ever lower in the horizon, taking on that faint reddish hue that promised a spectacular sunset.

The village itself looked rather eerily deserted. Probably it was the time of evening when most families were indoors eating, or preparing to go out and eat. As a result, she hardly saw a soul until she reached the inn. Which left her feeling vaguely disconnected, as if she was in one of those films where she was the sole survivor after some sort of apocalypse.

That feeling of aloneness was shattered, however, the moment she pushed through the inn doors and into the bar, which was full of people and the low hum of intense conversation.

The first person she saw was Min Buckey, sitting at the bar and drinking what looked like a large gin and tonic. Beside her, Silas watched her anxiously, barely sipping at a half-pint of what looked like cider.

Behind the bar, Richard Sparkey wiped some wine glasses clean with a spotless white cloth, and watched them a shade nervously. Further down the bar, Muriel was handing over a frothing pint of beer to Old Walter, who pounced on it with glee.

And there, sitting in Jenny's favourite window seat, was Dr Rory Gilchrist. Evidently, the woman in the trouser suit hadn't tracked him down, for he was placidly reading a local paper, and sipping from a glass containing what looked to Jenny like a shot of neat whisky.

There were a number of people sitting at the bar and tables, drinking and talking earnestly, and it was clear that the news had already travelled back to the inn. Which wasn't particularly surprising. Jenny knew that news in any village tended to travel faster than wildfire — and that bad news travelled fastest of all.

As she approached the bar, intending to order a big snifter of warming brandy to counteract her own case of mild shock, Richard straightened up slightly. 'So it's true then. Rachel Norman drowned?' he asked quietly, the moment she was within earshot.

'Yes,' she said curtly. 'I take it you and Muriel didn't come down to watch the show then?'

'Nah, too much clearing up to do here after lunch,' he said flatly. Which instantly reminded Jenny that she was supposed to be getting an evening supper ready for anyone who wanted it.

But she'd been kept for hours at the pond, and was now hopelessly behind schedule. When she said as much, to her intense relief Richard told her to forget it. Nobody would be expecting — or in the mood — to eat, he reasoned, and if anyone did want to, some cold meats and salad would just have to do them. 'Besides, I reckon all this lot,' and here he nodded at the crowd around him, 'have only come here to gossip, not eat, anyway,' he added morosely.

Jenny nodded gratefully and ordered a brandy. It was completely unlike her to not feel like getting to work in the kitchen, but the afternoon's events had completely taken it out of her. Her hands, as she reached for the drink, felt cold and a little numb.

'You look done in. Pretty grim, was it?' he asked, pushing the bulbous glass towards her.

Jenny nodded mutely, swirled the deep amber liquid in the bottom of the large glass and gratefully took a sip. Instantly as she felt the spirit slide down her throat, it began to warm her from the inside out. 'I expect the police will be along shortly,' she warned him wearily. 'They'll be wanting to speak to Min and Silas for sure, and everyone else who knew Rachel,' she added.

Again, Richard sighed. 'Not good for business, something like this,' he said quietly.

But Jenny thought, rather cynically, that it would probably have the opposite effect. Knowing human nature, customers would probably come flooding to the inn once the story hit the papers, eager to try and pick up the gossip first-hand, and see for themselves where the drowned woman had played the role of another drowned heroine.

With a non-committal grunt, Jenny took her brandy and made her way to the table nearest the window seat. As she sat down, she caught the Oxford don's eye, but Dr Gilchrist merely nodded at her curtly and went on reading his newspaper. Then she felt a movement behind her, and Rory's head came up. His gaze moved past her shoulder, and she saw his eyes widen slightly.

Jenny turned, half-expecting to see the woman in the trouser suit, but instead saw Vince Braine.

'Rory! I'm so glad I caught you here. I've just heard the most extraordinary thing! Is it true?' The country solicitor looked pale and a little harried as he joined his old friend on the window seat. In his hand he was carrying what looked like a vodka and tonic in a square glass. 'Is Rachel really dead?' he demanded.

'So it seems,' Rory said curtly. 'I was writing up that article I told you about in my room when the stragglers started to get back.' He nodded at the various members of the historical society and other audience members who were scattered around the bar area. 'So I came down and started picking up the gist of it from what I could overhear.'

'But it's . . . it's just unbelievable. What on earth happened?' Vince squeaked.

Rory shrugged impatiently. 'How the hell should I know? I wasn't even there. Sounds to me like she went in the water and must have had a heart attack or a stroke or something.'

'A heart attack? But Rachel was young and healthy. I never heard she had anything wrong with her heart.'

'Maybe it was something else then,' Rory said brusquely. 'Like I said, I wasn't there.' Then he said, a shade more kindly, 'I dare say the cause of death will be established sooner or later. They're bound to do an autopsy, after all.'

At this, Vince took a hasty sip from his glass. 'Poor Rachel,' he said. 'She was so lovely, wasn't she? And so full of plans for the future too. Oh Lord, how she went on about that commercial being her stepping stone to getting a part in one of the soaps,' he smiled fondly. 'And why not? Who's to say she wouldn't have made it big?' he demanded. 'Others before her have done just that. And now . . . It just doesn't bear thinking about. And now it makes me wonder . . .'

He left off, a strange look passing over his face.

And Jenny suddenly remembered the last time she'd heard Rachel and Vince speaking together. And what Rachel had asked the solicitor. And Jenny began to wonder too.

'Wonder what?' Rory said, again a shade brusquely.

'Oh nothing,' Vince said hastily. 'So, how are things now between you and Diana?' he rather clumsily changed the subject.

'That bloody woman just won't give up,' Rory exploded, then glanced hurriedly around the room and lowered his voice a shade. 'She's already tracked me down here — well, I told you about that. Do you know she's actually had a private investigator on to me? I mean, a bloody PI! I thought they only existed in bad American films.'

Vince sighed. 'Did she say what this investigator found out? Presumably she has no interest in, er . . . any lady friends you might have made since the divorce?'

Rory gave a snort of angry laughter. 'As if she cares about that! You know damn well what she's got this nosy bloody parker trying to root out. I told you — with Diana it's all about the money. As if she didn't bleed me dry in the divorce as it was.'

Vince Braine sighed and took another sip of his drink. 'Rory, you haven't done anything silly have you?' he asked so quietly that Jenny almost couldn't hear him.

'Silly? Me? I'm the least silly person I know,' Rory drawled.

'Now, Rory, don't go all sophisticated and witty on me,' Vince said sharply. 'I'm the one who handled your divorce, don't forget. And if Diana has any basis for her claims, then you're not the only one who'll be in hot water. Mud sticks, especially for people like me. Small firms like ours can't afford to be implicated in anything even remotely smacking of financial chicanery.'

'Don't be such a wimp, Vince. You know what Diana's like. A piranha in Prada! She's out for blood and my last pound of flesh. And as my solicitor, I'm relying on you to make sure she doesn't get it!'

'Yes, yes, that's all very well, but . . .' Vince began testily, when he suddenly broke off, and everything went quiet.

For a moment, Jenny was absurdly reminded of one of those old westerns, where a gunslinger pushes open the swing doors and walks in, and the piano player stops playing and everyone stops talking and turns to look at the new stranger in town.

But when Jenny glanced up and around, she didn't see a man in a cowboy outfit wearing a Stetson hat, but the slightly paunchy figure of Inspector Franklyn, and his attractive blonde-haired sergeant. They'd both just stepped through the open door and were looking around them with interest.

A moment later, the low buzz of conversation resumed, but everyone in the room was either openly or surreptitiously watching them.

But the inspector, it seemed, had eyes only for Min and Silas Buckey.

* * *

The American couple had changed out of their costumes, but with Min dressed in a flowing kaftan garment of purple with silver braiding and embroidery, and Silas dressed in khaki shorts with a polo shirt in moss green, both were radiating their nationality.

Jenny noticed Min's hand slip into that of her husband's as the policeman drew closer. And she saw Silas squeeze her hand back, silently offering comfort and support.

'Mr and Mrs Buckey, is it?' Franklyn asked mildly.

'Yes, that's us,' Silas responded at once, standing up from his bar stool and looking the Englishman straight in the eye. He also, Jenny noticed, moved his body slightly, half-blocking, half-sheltering Min from the inspector's eyeline.

Franklyn efficiently flipped open a little black leather wallet, showing his identification, and introduced himself. His sergeant did the same. 'I was wondering if I could have a quick word, sir,' Franklyn said politely. 'Perhaps down at the station?'

'I don't reckon we need to go to the police station, Inspector,' Silas said at once. 'It's not as if we've done anything wrong,' he added challengingly.

And Jenny could see at once that the large American was intent on being . . . if not exactly obstructionist, then determined not to let himself be bullied. He'd obviously had time to do some thinking, and must have realised, on hearing about Rachel's death, that he and his wife were sure to be quizzed. And had come to the conclusion that the only way to handle it was head on.

And Jenny, for one, couldn't help but feel like applauding his chutzpah.

Franklyn blinked, looking a little surprised by this blunt refusal.

'As you wish, sir,' he said a shade stiffly. 'Then perhaps we could go somewhere more private? Perhaps the landlord has a private study or . . .'

But again, Silas forestalled him. 'I can't see why we need privacy, Inspector. Neither my wife nor I have anything to hide.' He was speaking, Jenny was sure, as much to the crowded room as to the Inspector. 'We can speak here — can I get you a drink?' he offered amiably.

'No sir, not whilst I'm on duty,' Franklyn said, looking disconcerted by this unexpected turn of events. 'But are you sure you wouldn't rather do this in private?' he tried again.

'Do what?' Silas asked flatly.

'As you might be aware, sir, a young woman has died in rather unusual circumstances,' Franklyn said stiffly.

'Yes, we heard about Rachel,' Silas said, and sighed heavily. By now the whole room was clearly listening shamelessly, although pretending not to. And the female sergeant, for one, was clearly not happy about it, and kept shooting glances around the crowded bar.

But Jenny supposed that unless Inspector Franklyn wanted to arrest the Buckeys, there was no way he could insist on them going to the police station. And with him not even having established yet that a crime had actually taken place, he clearly wasn't able to do anything so formal as to make an arrest.

Besides, he was probably thinking that his superiors wouldn't be happy if he arrested some American tourists, only to have to release them with an apology later if it turned out Rachel's death had been due to natural causes. Creating diplomatic incidents with foreign nationals probably wouldn't look good on his personnel record.

Which left him with little choice but to play things Silas's way.

'And we were right sorry to hear about it, weren't we, Min?' the American swept on blithely. Beside him, Min, looking diminutive and pale, nodded silently. 'So if you've got questions for us, we'll be only too happy to answer them. Fire away.'

Franklyn, finally conceding to the inevitable, gave a weary sigh but nodded. 'Very well, sir. If that's what you want. As I understand it, you and your wife were part of the audience who followed Miss Norman as she made her way to the pond, yes?'

'Yeah, that's right. It was her big scene and everyone was looking forward to it, right, Min?'

Again, Min nodded without speaking.

'But when you got to the pond, just when Miss Norman got into the water, you started screaming, Mrs Buckey, is that right?' Franklyn asked, determined to get the woman speaking for herself, instead of merely nodding passively.

'Yes. I saw this enormous spider on me . . . crawling down my arm. I nearly died!' Min said. Her voice, when she finally spoke, was a mixture of horror and defiance. 'I hate spiders — you can ask anyone. Positively hate 'em!'

'Anyone can tell you that,' her husband took over once more. 'So I knocked it off her and tried to calm her down.

Then I took her back here,' Silas marched on. 'I made her a hot cup of tea up in our room, then we changed and came down here for something a bit stiffer. Richard here was kind enough to break open a bottle of Napoleon brandy, and we had a drink. It wasn't much after that when these good folks,' and here Silas looked around the room, as everyone in it tried to pretend that they weren't listening to every word he said, 'started coming back and we heard about the tragedy.'

'I see,' Franklyn said, a shade wryly. 'A very concise and quick account, Mr Buckey, thank you,' he added drolly. It had clearly not escaped him that the other man was trying to speed the process along and get things over with as quickly as possible. And Franklyn was just as determined not to let him. 'But perhaps we could get a few more details.' He showed his teeth briefly in what might have passed for a smile. 'Did you know Miss Norman well?'

'Hell no,' Silas protested. 'We only clapped eyes on her for the first time on Friday night, when this weekend shindig started.'

'And before that you were where?'

'London.'

'And Miss Norman was . . . friendly towards you?' Franklyn asked stiffly, very much aware of all the people around him listening with bated breath for the American's answer.

'Sure she was friendly, right, honey? All the am-dram people were. Like Sir Hugh over there,' Silas said evenly, nodding and then smiling over at Vince, who, suddenly finding himself the focus of all eyes, looked a bit like a rabbit caught in car headlights. 'And that young fellah that played Reginald Truby. All the actors were good sports and talked to us.'

Franklyn's lips twitched. Clearly here he had a worthy opponent, who wasn't going to be tripped up easily. Nevertheless he persevered gamely.

'I understand Miss Norman was a rather attractive young lady?' he tried next.

'Indeed she was,' Silas said. Too canny to deny it, and too smart not to see where this was heading, he made no move to try and demur, but neatly took the bull by the horns. 'From what I could tell, she and that fellah playing Reginald Truby had been an item at one time. And I think that Welsh fellah found her very attractive too. And why not? She was a glamorous actress. She was bound to turn heads — only natural, if you ask me.'

Franklyn acknowledged the neatness of this with a curt nod.

'So she definitely was flirtatious, would you say?'

Silas gave a man-of-the-world shrug and another broad smile. 'And why not? Nothing wrong with an attractive gal flirting is there, Inspector?'

'Not at all,' Franklyn said just as heartily. Two, after all, could play at this game! 'So long as men don't get the wrong idea. Take yourself for instance. A man of a certain age, shall we say? Did she flirt with you too?'

But Silas wasn't about to be put on the back foot so easily. 'Hell yes, son, of course she did. And I'd have felt insulted if she hadn't! We, along with everyone else staying here, paid good money for this Regency Extravaganza thing, and everyone was making sure we had a good time. Our landlord and landlady have been great, the food's been purely wonderful, and the amateur dramatics were a real treat. No doubt Rachel and all the others made it part of their job to be pleasant to us paying guests.'

Jenny bit back a grin and couldn't help but admire his stand. (Also, his comment about the food being purely wonderful hadn't gone unnoticed or unappreciated.) If Inspector Franklyn was intent on making something of Rachel's play for him, Silas was just as determined to play it all down.

'Min and me were saying only last night how much we were enjoying it all. Weren't we, honey?'

'Yes,' Min mumbled.

And, clearly sensing an easier target, Franklyn promptly turned his attention her way.

'But didn't you mind, Mrs Buckey?' he asked silkily. 'This attractive young actress flirting with your husband?'

But if he hoped that the American woman would break down, or make some kind of damning statement, he was doomed to disappointment. Like her husband, Min was made of sterner stuff.

'Oh no, Inspector, that would have been silly,' Min said, her chin coming up slightly. 'She was only doing her job, after all. And Silas wasn't the only man she flirted with. We all took it in good part. A bit of fun never hurt anyone.'

Franklyn, clearly frustrated by this reasonable rejoinder, nodded briskly. 'So it was all a harmless bit of fun was it?' he grated. 'You didn't feel at all threatened by it?'

'Goodness, Inspector, why would I? We're only here for the weekend, remember?' Min said innocently. 'Tomorrow Si and me are off to learn all about your William Shakespeare, up in Stratford-upon-Avon. And we wouldn't have seen Rachel, or any of these other good folks again,' Min pointed out with devastating logic, as she waved a hand around the room.

And Jenny had to acknowledge the truth of that with a small nod of her own.

For even *if* Rachel had been making a serious play for Silas Buckey, she'd only had a few hours in which to do so. And given that the Buckeys' marriage was clearly a happy one, and had been for the last twenty-five years, she could hardly have had time to present much of a threat.

Certainly not to the extent that Min would feel the need to kill her.

Besides, it was clear to everyone that she couldn't have done it. She simply hadn't had the opportunity. Nor had Silas, either, for at the time when Rachel Norman had been breathing her last, they'd had between twenty and thirty people looking right at them!

And as an alibi, that had to take some beating.

But then, Jenny had the feeling that the inspector wasn't thinking of them as being in the frame for the actual killing of the actress. But it was clear that Min's screaming fit had come at such an auspicious time. Whether intentional or not, the Buckeys had clearly provided a major distraction, just when it must have been most needed.

Which, Jenny thought grimly, begged an obvious question.

If Min, and maybe her husband, had deliberately created a diversion, *who* had they created it for? Who, in other words, was their accomplice?

And here, Jenny found herself stumped. For, as Min herself had just stated, the American couple didn't know anyone here! They had arrived in the village barely forty-eight hours previously.

But, just supposing for argument's sake that either Min or Silas together had decided that they needed to kill Rachel for some reason as yet totally unclear. Surely they couldn't have just stumbled upon *someone else* at the inn who also wanted her dead? The odds against that had to be astronomical. And although Jenny knew that sometimes in life really bizarre coincidences *could* happen, she just couldn't swallow it.

What's more, even if they *had* somehow discovered another enemy of Rachel's at the Regency Extravaganza, the Buckeys surely wouldn't have had enough time to convince this mythical other someone to join forces with them, thus risking life in prison, in a conspiracy to kill her. Why would the accomplice trust them?

Unless, of course, they'd met before.

Even given all these problems, Jenny nevertheless began a mental run-through of the list of candidates.

Ion Dryfuss. When would Min and Silas have had a chance to meet him? Their tour of Europe had definitely not included Wales yet — this much she knew from the Buckeys themselves, who were rather voluble about their travels, and themselves. (Which is how Jenny knew they'd not long celebrated their twenty-fifth wedding anniversary!)

Dr Rory Gilchrist? Well, Oxford wasn't that far away. And it was conceivable that they might have run into him in

London perhaps. But what did a distinguished academic and a wealthy American couple have in common?

The same went for Vince, or Matthew or anyone else in the am-dram society.

Unless, of course, chance had played no part in this at all? Jenny suddenly stiffened in her seat.

What if it had all been planned out well in advance? For all Jenny knew, Min and Silas and their as yet unknown conspirator might have been planning this for some time. Everyone here at the inn had given the impression that they didn't know one another before — but who could say whether that was true or not?

Jenny sighed in frustration. No doubt the inspector would have someone checking out the Buckeys' European itinerary thoroughly, as well as their backgrounds. And if some link could be found between the Buckeys and someone else here, then an arrest might well take place soon.

So why did Jenny think that was highly unlikely to happen?

* * *

Franklyn, after another ten frustrating minutes questioning the Buckeys and getting no further forward, finally drew the interview to a close and glanced around the room for further victims.

There was a concerted bobbing movement as virtually everyone in the room tucked their heads down and became very interested in their drinks.

Consulting his notebook, Franklyn whispered something to his sergeant, who glanced around, and then nodded over at Jenny.

Or rather, at the two men seated behind her.

'Oh hell, looks like we're next, Vince,' she heard Dr Rory Gilchrist drawl dryly. 'Feeling up for the third degree?'

The country solicitor snorted. 'There'll be nothing of the kind — at least not as far as *I'm* concerned,' Vince Braine said, his voice sounding grim and not a little huffy. 'And I have to say, I think Mr Buckey was most unwise to insist on being questioned in public! That's most uncalled for, I think. I'm surprised the inspector allowed it.'

'Oh, I don't know, I think it showed a certain devil-may-care flair,' the Oxford academic said with a smile, clearly slipping into the role of devil's advocate with relish. But probably more out of professional habit, Jenny judged, than with any real conviction in what he was saying. She suspected that Rory Gilchrist spent so much of his time in learned debate at his college, both with his fellow dons and with his students, that he was probably unable to do anything else, even in his down time.

'Our American friend was playing to the room as much as the inspector,' he continued expansively, 'and who can blame him? The moment they came into the room they singled him and his wife out. It was clear to everyone that he was in the firing line, and that has to make a man's hackles rise. He was just making it clear to everyone that he had nothing to hide. That's just a normal human reaction, isn't it? Nobody wants their peers to start looking at them as if they're beyond the pale.'

'Hmph! The jails are probably full of people who thought they had nothing to hide and were soon proved how wrong they were,' the older man shot back, sounding less than convinced. 'We don't have a right to remain silent in this country for nothing,' he continued grimly. 'If only people would have the good sense to use it more often! But they're afraid to, that's the problem. The police make them think that they'll look guilty if they refuse to speak.'

Oh dear, Jenny thought, hiding a smile. It sounded very much as if the legal eagle was getting on his high horse. No doubt when it came to am-dram Vince was willing to play second fiddle, but when it came to matters within his own area of expertise he was going to be a stickler for the rules.

And she thought, as she watched the two police officers approach them, that Inspector Franklyn and his pretty sergeant were going to get rather short shrift here.

And right on cue, she heard Vince say sternly, 'If you'll take my advice, Rory, you won't say anything without your solicitor present.'

Rory gave a small smile. 'You *are* my solicitor, Vince,' he pointed out dryly.

'I *was*, in the matter of your divorce,' Vince said, lowering his voice now as the two police officers were almost upon them. 'But I'm not now, unless you officially engage me. But after what happened last time, I'm not sure if—' He broke off abruptly as Franklyn's shadow loomed over them and it became clear that he could now hear what they were saying.

Jenny obligingly hitched her chair around a little, giving the police officers better access to the window seat. And she wasn't surprised when the inspector nodded his thanks at her, selected one of the chairs that had been pushed under her table, and drew it up a little closer to the two men, giving them the illusion of privacy.

The sergeant, Jenny noticed, remained standing, leaning unobtrusively against the wall, and was quick to flip out her notebook.

'Good evening, gentlemen,' Franklyn began amiably enough, turning first to look at Rory Gilchrist. 'I take it you're the Dr Gilchrist who's currently staying at a room in this inn, sir?'

'Guilty as charged, officer,' Rory said with a bright smile, making the older man beside him wince.

'This is no time for levity, Rory,' Vince Braine chided sharply. 'Poor Rachel's dead, remember!'

'No. Of course, you're right.' The academic had the grace to flush slightly, and lifting his glass of whisky gave it a slight shake. 'Sorry, I think I've had a bit more to drink than I should have.' Although who he was apologising to — his friend or Inspector Franklyn — was rather hard to distinguish.

'That's quite all right, sir,' Franklyn put in smoothly. 'I'm sure the events of the day have been a shock for you all. And a little snifter of what you fancy doesn't necessarily hurt, in the circumstances.'

And, Jenny thought with a silent smile of inner amusement, if the Oxford don became a little squiffy and started blurting out his secrets, Inspector Franklyn wasn't going to complain.

'Yes, er . . . yes,' Rory agreed, a shade uncertainly now. 'I didn't know her well, obviously, but it's still a tragedy when one so young and beautiful dies, isn't it?'

'Ah, so you and Miss Norman weren't friends then?' the inspector put in silkily.

Rory looked genuinely startled by the question. 'What? No, of course not. Why should we be?' And then he frowned aggressively. 'And if someone's been telling you differently, Inspector, then I'm afraid you've been misled. Until I arrived here on Friday evening, I'd never met Miss Norman.'

'No need to get upset, sir,' Franklyn smiled at him wolfishly. 'Nobody has said that you were close. No, I was just wondering, sir, why a man of your, er, stature and learning, and coming from so close by, like, booked for this weekend at all? I mean,' he continued, noting that his witness had begun to flush uncomfortably, 'it just struck me that it was kind of odd. Leaving Oxford, which isn't that far from here, in order to spend three nights away, when you could easily commute it.' Franklyn sighed and shook his head. 'It didn't make much sense. Especially when all the others are from much further away, which *does* makes sense. Mr Dryfuss all the way from Wales, and Mr and Mrs Buckey from across the ocean.'

Franklyn paused to scratch his nose portentously. 'You expect people to go some distance away if they're going to bother to take a break, don't you?' And not giving Dr Gilchrist time to respond to this, he then swept on ruthlessly, 'And to go in for a bit of amateur theatricals, telling a tale that seems to me to be rather more fictional than historical . . . well, it just didn't seem to me to be the sort of thing a man like you would be interested in. If you see what I mean, sir.'

Beside him, Vince Braine shifted uncomfortably, and Rory gave a wry smile. No doubt, Jenny thought with a pang of sympathy, the Oxford man was beginning to wish he'd taken his friend's advice and kept his mouth shut!

But, having embarked on answering the inspector's questions, he couldn't very well change course now without appearing to have something to hide, Jenny mused. So perhaps there was some merit behind the trial-by-public-opinion method that the policeman had stumbled upon?

'In that you're quite right, Inspector. I can't say that the rather dubious tale of Lady Hester and her young lover was of much interest to me,' Rory confirmed, sighing heavily.

'Ah.'

'However,' Rory swept on smoothly, 'the local eye-catcher that they have here *is* very much of interest. What's more, they are something of a hobby of mine, Inspector. So when I saw this weekend advertised, it looked like a good opportunity to leave Oxford and all her many distractions behind, and settle down to write a nice little article about it, in peace and quiet.'

Jenny noticed that Sergeant O'Connor frowned very slightly over the word 'eyecatcher' as she was scribbling away in her notes, and realised that here was someone else who had no idea what it meant — which made her feel, a little shamefully, rather pleased.

Clearly Sergeant O'Connor's immediate senior didn't know what it was either, for Franklyn's next question was a simple repeat of the word.

'Eyecatcher?'

Rory smiled. 'The Faltringham Eyecatcher to be exact, Inspector. It lies barely two miles outside the village on the estate of the Faltringham family. Who had it built back in 1742.' Rory leaned back in his chair a bit, and clearly relished delivering a short lecture. This, after all, was well within his comfort zone, and allowed him to take a break from being on the receiving end of so many pertinent questions.

'Back in those days, Inspector, the landed gentry had money to burn, and a near inexhaustible supply of labour, such that they could pay peanuts. Consequently, they spent their money freely on all the latest fashions and fads, regard-less of what they were, in order to display their status in a game of one-upmanship with their neighbours. And one of the best ways of showing off was to landscape vast amounts of their lands to complement their more formal gardens, adding lakes, grottoes and especially small buildings. And in the case of the Faltringham eyecatcher, this consisted of having three great stonking arches built, in the local stone, right on the crest of a hill in direct line with Faltringham House. Thus giving their guests a "vista" to look at far beyond the bound-ary of the rose gardens and more formal areas surrounding the house.'

'A sort of folly, you mean,' Franklyn interrupted some-what impatiently, sounding deeply unimpressed. 'Like those little domed pagodas and temple-thingies you see in big fancy gardens?'

'Not quite, Inspector, but in that area,' Rory corrected him with an amiable smile — as he might a less-than-bright student. 'A folly can be anything, from a grotto to a tower or a temple-thingy as you so rightly say, but it could be placed anywhere — in a stand of trees, say, or in a hollow, or any-where else out of sight. A grotto, by its very nature, would be in a cave, for instance, or underground. But an eyecatcher was something specifically built out in the open, in order to catch the eye. Specifically so that the ladies and gentlemen of the time would have something to see in the distance. In this case, three stone arches built to mimic a ruined priory or abbey perhaps. To give the illusion of gothic, romantic ruins.'

'Ah,' the inspector said, still sounding less than impressed.

Jenny nodded to herself and had to smile. Once explained, an eyecatcher seemed rather self-explanatory!

'It was actually a fascinating craze, and for an historian like me, naturally, it was of interest. That's where I was this afternoon, in fact,' Rory swept on, now raising his own voice a little, in the manner of Silas Buckey. And, like the American, was stating his alibi loud and clear for all those listening to hear.

Just like Silas, he didn't want any nasty rumours spreading around that might connect him to a dead, pretty young actress. Men such as himself, a professional with a reputation to guard and a social standing to uphold, had to be careful, after all.

'I had no interest in watching the amateur dramatics, but I was interested in photographing the eyecatcher to go with the article I was writing for a history periodical that I subscribe to, and occasionally write for.'

The inspector sighed softly. 'So you were nowhere near the village pond this afternoon Dr Gilchrist?'

'No, I wasn't,' Rory said flatly and loudly.

'Er, did you go to this eyecatcher alone?'

Rory smiled thinly. 'Yes, Inspector.'

'And did anyone see you at this eyecatcher, sir?'

'Hardly, Inspector. It's just a pile of stones in the middle of a farmer's field. I dare say a few sheep might vouch for me, if you care to question them.'

Someone in a far corner tittered at this, but the inspector ignored this magnificently.

'And what time did you go to see this folly, sir?'

'I left here straight after lunch. Say between two-thirty and three o'clock, I imagine. I wasn't paying much attention to the time, you understand? I had no reason to.'

'Yes, sir. And you returned when, do you think?'

Rory made a show of glancing at his watch now. 'I must have got back here a little before five-thirty I would think. Or maybe a bit later? Richard might know.'

'Richard? Oh, Mr Sparkey, the landlord?'

'Yes. He served me a drink at the bar.'

'Very good, sir, I'll check with him later. Now, I've heard that Miss Norman was a very friendly young lady, sir. A bit flirtatious, one might say. Did you and she . . .'

'No,' Rory said flatly and uncompromisingly. Beside him, Vince Braine sighed heavily. Rory ignored him.

'Did you ever see or hear her arguing with anybody, sir?' Franklyn pressed on.

'I can't say as I did.'

'And you're not aware of any incident involving the young lady that you think should be drawn to our attention?'

'As I told you, Inspector,' the academic said patiently, 'I wasn't really interested in the theatrical aspect of the weekend. I barely paid any of the players any attention at all. Apart from my friend Vincent here, of course.'

'Hmm,' the inspector said thoughtfully, catching Jenny's eye.

He knew, of course, because Jenny had filled him in on all that she'd seen and heard, that the Oxford don had been arguing with another woman. But since that woman hadn't — yet — turned up dead, he couldn't see how it was really relevant.

Nevertheless, he decided to poke around it a little, just to see what came of it. Inspector Franklyn rather liked being a nuisance to those who thought themselves his betters — either by dint of earning more money than he did, or because they thought themselves either morally or intellectually superior.

'I understand that you met an old friend here at the inn, sir.'

'What?' Rory asked, stiffening slightly and casting a quick, suspicious look at Vince, who looked as surprised by the question as Dr Gilchrist.

'A rather attractive red-headed woman in a trouser suit. You were seen, er . . . talking in an animated way with her?'

'Oh. Diana,' Rory said shortly, sighing heavily. 'That was just my ex-wife, Inspector. And nothing at all to do with this,' and he waved a hand vaguely around the room.

In her seat, Jenny tensed. She'd have to tell the inspector that Diana Gilchrist *had* been at the pond this afternoon — and, what's more, had been rather anxious not to be questioned by the police. But since she was fairly sure that he'd want that information kept private, she couldn't just blurt it out here and now.

'I see, sir,' the inspector nodded thoughtfully. 'Well, that will be all for now, Dr Gilchrist. But if anything else occurs to you concerning Miss Norman, you will notify me at once?'

'Of course,' Rory said, clearly looking relieved that it was all over. And reaching for his glass, he tossed back his remaining whiskey with a gulp.

The inspector then turned to the older man beside him. 'And you are Mr Vincent Braine, I understand? And you're also a member of the Amateur Dramatic Society, and performed here over the weekend?'

'I am, Inspector, but I have to say, I don't think this is any way to conduct an interview, and I, for one, shall not be saying anything further!'

CHAPTER NINE

Inspector Franklyn, perhaps not unexpectedly, blinked a little at both the abruptness and implied antagonism of this statement. After enduring both Silas's and Dr Gilchrist's insistence on being upfront and open about things in front of so many witnesses, he felt himself now being wrong-footed by the distinctly confrontational attitude of the older, eminently respectable-looking man glowering back at him.

'Of course, sir,' he began cautiously and soothingly. 'That is certainly your right, and—'

'I'm very aware that that is my right, Inspector,' Vince interrupted him crisply. 'I'm a senior partner at Braine, Phipps and Bagley, which is one of several solicitors' offices that provides services to the local area,' Vince couldn't resist a bit of free advertising.

'Ah,' the inspector said, suddenly seeing the light. And abruptly changed gears. 'At last, a man who understands the law,' he said with a beatific smile. 'In that case, sir, I'll simply ask you for a few necessary details and then move on. Your full name please, sir?'

Vince, unable to refuse such a simple request, rather grumpily condescended to give his name, then his address.

'And just to make sure I've got this right,' Franklyn slipped in craftily, 'you were playing the part of . . .' the inspector made a big show of consulting his notebook, 'Sir Hugh, opposite Miss Norman, who played your wife, so to speak?'

'Yes, I had that privilege,' Vince agreed stiffly. 'Rachel was a very fine actress, Inspector. We Caulcott Deeping Players were lucky to have her join us.'

'Oh? She was a bit of a star was she?'

'She was the only one of us who had professional connections, yes. She'd done some advertising work. And she had a wonderful voice. You may have heard it on several voice-overs . . .' Vince, suddenly aware that he was, indeed, actually answering the inspector's questions in public, suddenly closed his mouth with a snap and glared at him. 'Once again, Inspector, I have to remind you that the proper and rightful place for me to give a statement of this kind is at the police station.'

'Sorry, yes! Of course, sir — so when can you come in?' Franklyn asked, all wide-eyed innocence. 'Naturally, we'd like to get as much done as soon as possible. But I'm aware that your time must be valuable?'

Vince flushed at this. Clearly he didn't like the implication that he accorded his free time as being more important than co-operating after the death of a young woman. 'I can come in tomorrow morning, first thing. Say nine-thirty?' he said, through slightly gritted teeth.

'Wonderful, sir,' the inspector said fulsomely. 'Sergeant, we have all the details of Miss Norman's home address and next of kin, don't we? Because if not, I'm sure Mr Braine wouldn't mind giving them to us.'

'Yes, sir, we have them,' O'Connor said flatly. 'The family liaison officer should be informing her parents by now.'

Again Vince flushed angrily. Now he was being portrayed as a nit-picking boor in the face of a genuine tragedy. As if he didn't feel deeply for the girl's poor parents!

'Fine, fine,' Franklyn said with a heavy sigh.

'Look, Inspector, I have as much feeling for Rachel's family as anyone,' Vince began hotly. 'What happened to her was an absolute tragedy.'

'Yes, sir. And I expect you'd feel it deeply, too, since you'd known her for some time?'

'Nearly three years, yes.'

'So this Regency play wasn't the first time you'd worked with her?'

'Good grief, no!'

'Was it going well, would you say, sir? The role of . . . Lady Hester, wasn't it? Did Miss Norman seem to be enjoying it?'

'Yes, I think so,' Vince said, clearly being a little economical with the truth now. Jenny had already told the inspector that the dead woman had thought the little production was way beneath her.

'So she seemed very much as normal, would you say?'

Vince bridled. 'Certainly she did, Inspector.'

'But I understand that last night, just before you gave your evening performance here at the inn, Miss Norman asked you a rather startling question, didn't she, sir?' Franklyn slipped in effortlessly.

Vince startled like a horse having a firework thrown under its legs. 'What? What do you mean? Certainly not!' he denied hotly.

'Oh?' Franklyn made a good show of looking puzzled. And again, ostentatiously consulted his notebook. Meanwhile the rest of the avidly listening room held its collective breath.

'I've been told, by several witnesses,' Franklyn added the lie smoothly, 'that Miss Norman asked you whether or not it was true that if somebody knew of something illegal happening, and that person didn't then disclose it, that they could be held accountable for it under the law?'

It took a moment for Vince, and everyone else, to untangle this rather convoluted sentence.

And then, for a moment, there was a tense, expectant silence.

And Jenny had the sudden but overwhelming feeling that somebody, somewhere in the room, had suddenly become very frightened indeed. In fact, out of the corner of her eye, she just caught a sudden, sharp, compulsive movement, almost as if someone had jerked, as if being given an electric shock.

But when she quickly turned her head and looked around the room, she couldn't tell who it might have been. Her eyes flickered briefly over Silas and Min, but they seemed to be sipping their drinks placidly at the bar.

Then, with a start, she noticed that Ion Dryfuss was sitting at the stool beside them. And just when had he slipped in, Jenny wondered. He must have come back not long after she had, for he'd now obviously showered and changed into dry clothes.

But when had he come downstairs from his room? And just how much had he heard of the inspector's rather unorthodox questioning of his fellow weekenders?

'Well, er, she might have done something of the kind,' Vince's reluctant voice suddenly dragged Jenny back to the drama going on right beside her, and she turned her attention back to the inspector's deft handling of the old solicitor.

She looked at Vince thoughtfully. Was there more behind his unwillingness to talk to the police than mere pedantry?

'And what did you advise her, sir? As a man of the law, I'm sure you were able to give her chapter and verse?' Franklyn flattered him cheerfully.

'Well, I didn't really have the time to go into it then and there, because we were just about to start our performance, and that area of the law can be a rather complicated matter that would depend very much on circumstances,' Vince spluttered. 'But naturally the question alarmed and rather concerned me. It could have been nothing, or equally, it could have been a serious matter, obviously, and I definitely needed to know more details, which was why I intended to talk to her more fully later when . . . Now look here, Inspector,' Vince, for a second time becoming aware that he'd allowed the inspector to lead him astray, got up abruptly from his seat. 'As I told you at the outset, this is not the time or place to discuss such things! I'll see you at the police station tomorrow morning at nine-thirty sharp, where I'll be very happy to answer any and all questions, and make and sign my statement. Now, if you don't mind, I think I'll get home to bed. It's been a long and tiring and, quite frankly, very distressing day. So I'll bid you good night.'

And so saying, he walked stiffly out of the now totally silent room, a slight flush on his cheeks at being the centre of so much intense attention.

Jenny heard the inspector sigh heavily as he left. Franklyn then turned to his sergeant and nodded. 'Right then. We seem to have spoken to all the main players now — in a manner of speaking. Is there anyone else that we need to get to tonight who can't wait until tomorrow?' he asked wearily.

The blonde woman nodded. 'We should probably talk to Matthew Greenslade, sir. The other major actor in the drama,' she added, when he looked at her a shade blankly.

'Oh, the young man who was playing the doomed lover,' Franklyn rolled his eyes. 'OK. Let's get to it, then we'll call it a night. He's not here is he?' he added, looking around the room hopefully.

'No, sir,' Sergeant O'Connor said. 'He wasn't at the performance, it seems.'

Franklyn nodded gloomily. 'But he lives locally I hope?'

'Cheltenham, sir, not far,' Lucy said encouragingly. 'I'll drive, shall I?' she added more firmly.

And suddenly, the bar room began to fill with excited chatter as the two police officers left.

'Bloody hell, I need another drink,' she heard Rory Gilchrist mutter from his position on the window seat.

Jenny thought that she could probably do with another one herself! It was barely eight o'clock, after all, and the rest of the evening was stretching out ahead of her.

* * *

As Lucy O'Connor drove them quickly but competently towards the town of Cheltenham, famous for its horse racing

126

and a rather distinguished ladies' college, Thomas Franklyn did a mental recap of the last few hours. It was something he often did once the shape of his latest task became clear, and it helped him sort out his priorities and get things clear in his head.

So, how was this latest case shaping up? Mentally, he gave a little grunt. Until he had the results of the autopsy, he wasn't even sure that he *had* much of a case at all. Despite the super-doc's doubts, it could all turn out to be a death due to natural causes. In which case he could pass it on to the coroner and say good riddance to it.

But somehow he didn't think that was likely. And when he tracked down the reason for this belief, he realised that it had less to do with the medical examiner's doubts, and more to do with the attitude of one Miss Jenny Starling!

Because the cook, he could tell, definitely thought the young girl had been murdered. And whilst the opinion of a member of the public shouldn't have amounted, as Humphrey Bogart would have insisted, to 'a hill of beans,' in this case, it very much did. For, after knowing her less than a few hours, the inspector was beginning to experience, first-hand, the reasons why some of his colleagues regarded her with such a mixture of high esteem and extreme displeasure!

The woman clearly saw and understood the things that happened around her. And if she felt something was off, then it probably was.

Franklyn sighed, watching the darkening scenery flash by outside the car window.

Without doubt, the cook's witness testimony so far had been very helpful, as had her verbal sketches of all the people involved. Which, after seeing and talking to the majority of them for himself now, he rather thought were spot on. So he was fairly confident that he had a good basic background knowledge of both the crime scene and the cast of characters — so to speak — that were involved.

Apart from the man they were about to see, that is.

'So what do we know about this Greenslade bloke then, Lucy?' he asked quietly.

Sergeant O'Connor, a very smooth and efficient driver, never took her eyes off the road, but recounted what she'd been able to glean about the am-dram actor over the course of the afternoon and evening — both from talking to people and accessing her laptop.

'Matthew Greenslade, sir. Aged twenty-five, went to Reading Uni where he took a BA in . . . damn! I forget. Something general, sir — business studies I think. Anyway, he's still up to his ears in student debt. Six one, with blond hair and green eyes, clean driving licence. He's not known to us,' Lucy added, giving the usual shorthand phrase for saying that he had no criminal record or convictions. 'He works in an estate agent's in Cheltenham, but still lives with his mum and dad, apparently.' Her voice became a shade dry at the irony of this statement.

'Poor sod, I bet he takes some stick from his friends for that,' Franklyn muttered sympathetically.

'Yes, sir,' Lucy said flatly. 'As you know, it's hard for young people like us to get on the housing ladder. Apparently he's saving for a deposit for a flat in one of those new-builds on the edge of town — with his firm's help, naturally. But that might all be falling by the wayside, now that he and his fiancée seem to have parted. She was probably going halves with the mortgage plan.'

Franklyn grunted. 'Who is she again?'

'Felicity Thornton, sir, a hairdresser at a local salon. Again, not known to us.'

Her superior officer sighed and turned his attention back to the night flashing past his passenger-side window, and neither of them spoke again until Lucy's satnav helpfully deposited them outside a modest but well-maintained semi. Set in the middle of a cul-de-sac of similar houses, which had clearly been built just after the Second World War by the local council for returning soldiers, it had grey plastered walls and newly installed white PVC double glazing.

The front garden was small but looked tidy, with a little magnolia tree set in the middle of a pocket-handker-chief-sized lawn.

'Very nice,' Lucy said, getting out and looking around. Unlike new-builds, which seemed to her to have a shelf-life of about five minutes, these old council houses had been built to last, by proper craftsmen who knew what they were doing. Not that many of them belonged to the housing association anymore, she supposed, since it was clear that the majority of them were now in private ownership. Extensions, conversions, and conservatories sprouted here and there like so many mushrooms.

Like the man they were here to see, Lucy too was having trouble getting into her first home, and still shared a two-bedroom flat in Gloucester with a girl she'd known since her schooldays.

They walked up the front path, which was bordered by two strips of neatly clipped, low box hedging, and rang the doorbell. The man who answered was clearly not Matthew Greenslade, being somewhere in his late fifties, but was almost certainly his father. Tall and fair, he looked troubled by finding two police officers on his doorstep on a Sunday evening. As well he might.

'We were hoping to have a few words with your son Matthew, sir,' Franklyn said, after displaying his identification card. 'It's just routine,' he added blandly.

'But what's it about?' Greenslade senior demanded, looking more worried than aggressive. 'He's not in trouble is he?'

'No, sir, not at all. We just need to ask him a few questions concerning an incident that occurred this afternoon.' Franklyn was at his most reassuring.

'When this afternoon? Only our Matt has been in all day. Moping, if you ask me. He and his girl have had a row, you see.'

'Yes, sir. Up in his room, is he?' Franklyn pressed, shifting his balance slightly forward, and was relieved when the other man reluctantly stepped back to let them into the small hallway.

'Yes, upstairs, first door on the left,' Mr Greenslade admitted, nodding at the staircase. And then watched them go up the stairs with a worried frown creasing his forehead. From further inside the house, both the police officers clearly heard a woman's querulous voice asking what was going on.

Both of them hoped the parents wouldn't come knocking on their son's door to offer support and satisfy their curiosity.

When Franklyn first tapped on the bedroom door Mr Greenslade had indicated, he could hear nothing at all; no sense of movement, furtive or otherwise. A shade impatiently, he tapped again, more sharply this time, and was finally rewarded with the unmistakable sound of a bedspring complaining. A moment later the door opened.

The young man who slouched in the doorway looking out at them needed a shave, and had eyes that could only be described as bleary. What's more, a definite aroma of alcohol wafted from him as he abruptly straightened up.

'What the hell? Who are you?'

Lucy eyed the tall, square-jawed handsome young man and felt herself perk up a bit. She'd always been partial to a man with a nice square jaw and Hollywood leading-man good looks! She could quite see why a man like this had joined an am-dram society.

'Police, sir,' Franklyn said, once again showing his ID. 'Can we have a quick word?' And not giving him the chance to say no, took a step forward, forcing the younger man to retreat back into a modest-sized bedroom.

Lucy followed him in and firmly shut the door behind her — just in case the parents came sneaking up the stairs in an attempt to eavesdrop.

Once it had accommodated a double bed, Matthew Greenslade's room had a small space left over for a large, old-fashioned wooden wardrobe stuck in one corner, and a set of drawers in another. An old armchair had been requisitioned from downstairs and had been set to one side of the room's only window, and in front of it had been placed a tiny coffee table that probably caught your shins every time you went past it. A small television set had been positioned on the wall opposite the bed, and rested a shade precariously on black iron brackets.

'Sorry, but there's nowhere much to sit,' Matthew muttered, clearly confused by their presence. 'Er, I don't mind if you sit on the edge of the bed,' he added, slumping back down on the bed himself.

Lucy, in the pursuit of the proper decorum, elected to sit on the only chair, whilst Franklyn decided to simply stand, leaning one shoulder comfortably against a wall and eyeing the young man thoughtfully.

On the floor beside the bed were what looked like half a dozen or so empty bottles of beer. Which probably accounted for the scent of booze.

'Been having a bit too much to drink, sir?' he asked mildly.

Matthew flushed. 'Yeah. I suppose I have a bit. I don't normally drink this much,' the words were just slightly slurred, but he sounded sober enough to know what he was saying. 'Only I've had a major barney with my girlfriend . . . well, not my girlfriend any longer, I suppose, and . . . Sorry, but this can't be . . . I mean, why are you here exactly?'

But Franklyn wasn't in a forthcoming mood.

'Your girlfriend — this would be Miss Thornton, would it? Felicity Thornton?' he asked, not because he needed the clarification, but just because he wanted to set a pattern: he asked a question, Matthew answered it. Simple as that.

'Yeah? How do you know Flick?' the young man asked, sounding astonished, and as if willing to believe that the forces of law and order really did see and know all. Had he been a little bit more sober, he might have been less easily impressed.

'And she was more than your girlfriend, I believe? You were engaged to be married, in fact?' Franklyn pressed on.

'Right,' Matthew admitted, looking more and more bewildered. 'Well, we were, but that's all off now. When she called and asked if she could come around after Sunday lunch today, I thought for a minute that she might want to patch things up. But it was only to give me the ring back.'

It was only then that Franklyn noticed a small gold and diamond ring resting on the tiny bedside table beside a digital alarm clock and his wristwatch. (Lucy O'Connor had spotted it straight away, naturally.)

'Ah, hard luck, sir,' Franklyn said. 'And I take it the reason for the, er, break-up was your affair with Rachel Norman?'

Again Matthew Greenslade flushed angrily. 'I don't see what this has to do with . . . You're the police, right? What did I do?'

'I don't know, sir, what *did* you do?' Franklyn asked with a wide smile.

Matthew sighed and ran a hand across his face. 'I really need a kip,' he said heavily. 'My brain seems to have gone AWOL. I don't understand . . . What are you doing here?'

Franklyn nodded crisply. 'Right you are, sir, let's get down to brass tacks. Can you tell me where you were today, between, say, two-thirty and five-thirty?'

Matthew sighed. 'Here. Like I said. Flick came over. We had a big barney, she flung the ring in my face and left, saying this time it was for good. And I . . .' He nodded down at the empty beer bottles around him. 'Drowned my sorrows, as you can see.'

Lucy winced slightly at the word 'drowned' but made a note of his reply in her notebook without comment.

'Can anyone corroborate that, sir?' Franklyn asked flatly.

'What? Why would they need to?' And then, looking up and seeing the set expression on the older man's face, Matthew seemed to shrink his head back into his shoulders a little, rather like a tortoise, and mumbled, 'I dunno. My mum and dad can, probably.'

'They were up here in your room with you?' Franklyn asked facetiously.

'No, course they weren't,' Matthew snapped, flushing a little in embarrassment. 'But they'd have heard me if I had left,' he insisted.

'Sergeant, just nip downstairs will you, and see if either Mr or Mrs Greenslade left the house themselves this afternoon. Or heard their son do so.'

'Yes, sir,' Lucy said smartly, and slipped out quietly.

Matthew watched her go with some alarm, not at all sure he wanted to be left alone with her intimidating superior. Swallowing hard, he looked back at Franklyn.

'Why do you want to know where I was this afternoon?' he finally plucked up the courage to ask.

'Because this afternoon, Rachel Norman died,' Franklyn replied flatly.

For a moment, the handsome face looking up at him didn't seem to react to this portentous statement at all. Then he saw the black pupils in the pale blue, slightly bloodshot eyes contract, and the colour bleached from his cheeks.

'Rachel's *dead?*'

* * *

Back in the car ten minutes later, Franklyn sighed wearily. 'I take it the parents backed up his story?' he asked his sergeant.

'Yes, sir. His father mowed the lawn around four, but his mother was in the living room all the time. They heard the argument between Felicity and their son, and knew that after she'd left he'd raided the fridge for some beer, but just decided to let him get on with things. They're both adamant he never left the house.'

'Hmmm,' Franklyn said. Lucy didn't need telling that, as an alibi, parents weren't always the most trustworthy of witnesses. He'd known mothers of even the most hardened of criminals swear that their dear little darlings were with them when they knew damned well that they weren't.

'Did you believe them?' he asked vaguely.

'Yes, sir,' Lucy said.

'Hmmm,' Franklyn said again. 'And we've no sightings of him from anyone at the pond?'

'No, sir. We've got nothing that puts him at the scene.'

'Pity. Of all the people we've questioned so far, he seems to have the best motive for wanting the girl dead. Well, him and the Welsh chap, perhaps. OK, so we scratch Matthew Greenslade off the list. Provisionally, anyway.'

'Yes, sir. You want to interview Felicity Thornton while we're here? She only lives about ten minutes away.'

Franklyn sighed. 'Might as well, I suppose. It'll save us a job tomorrow anyway.'

CHAPTER TEN

Back at the Spindlewood Inn, Malcolm McFadden was trying manfully to keep a cheerful expression on his face as he stood drinking at the bar, but it wasn't that easy.

In his mid-fifties, Malcolm was a tall, lean man, with a head of thick and luxuriant white hair (about which he was secretly very vain) and thick white eyebrows over dark brown eyes. He had a prominent, what he liked to call a Roman nose, and was wearing his usual 'working' outfit of black trousers, with a dark shirt and lightweight black overcoat.

He dressed like this because he liked to 'disappear' into the dark as much as possible when he gave his guided ghost walks, since it all added to the atmosphere.

Malcolm lived in a village about ten miles away, and had been somewhat unexpectedly and summarily 'retired' from his job in the city when the last economic bust had hit rather closer to home than all the previous busts had done. Luckily though, he'd invested wisely during the boom years, and since his redundancy had also come with a rather nice golden handshake, he had at least been left financially secure. Not so luckily, he had very quickly become bored out of his mind.

Needless to say, Sylvia, his wife of some nearly twenty-five years, used to her own circle of friends and activities, had not been pleased to suddenly find him under her feet all day long, with a face like a long wet weekend.

Sweetly, she had advised him to find a hobby. And since he was not the kind of man to spend his days in an allotment shed, had instead turned the attic of his house into an office, and had set about writing 'that book' that he'd always promised himself he would write one day.

But, it quickly transpired, his was not the kind of mind that easily turned to fiction, and for a while he'd groped unsuccessfully to find a subject that caught his imagination. After a lifetime working with banks and sorting out various financial portfolios he wanted nothing more to do with business. Besides, only a boring old fart would write a book nobody would want to read about economics. Alas, he knew nothing about gardening, stamp collecting or bird watching either.

It had been during a visit to his local library in search of inspiration that he'd come across a slim volume, written in the twenties by a local historian, detailing the circumstances surrounding a famous nearby 'haunted vicarage.' This unhappy house had been made briefly famous back in the day, after the spectacular murder/suicide of a resident vicar and his wife.

Curious, Malcolm had read it, been intrigued, and since then had never looked back, doing his own research and unearthing several other 'haunted' houses in the local area. Although not a believer himself, he found people's willingness to believe in the supernatural fascinating, and thus had the topic for his book at last.

Alas, Malcolm's book, now five years in the writing, had yet to get past chapter three. But Malcolm's trawl of the internet in search of 'facts' had led him to visit various 'ghost walk' websites, such as the famous ones in Edinburgh and London, and had sparked another idea in his head.

Why not set up his very own Cotswold ghost walk? The area was full of tourists (or punters, as he often thought of them in his more cynical moments) and thus, he reasoned, he wouldn't be short of clients. Plus, he quickly discovered that actually talking to people was far more pleasing and satisfying than sitting alone in his attic office and sweating over a recalcitrant laptop. The written word, he'd often found, could be far more elusive than the spoken one.

Furthermore, he had to admit that talking as 'the expert' to a small group of interested acolytes was far more gratifying — and mirrored his previous career in banking — than life as a solitary, underappreciated author!

Of course, he didn't need the income as such, which was why he only charged a modest fee, which in turn virtually guaranteed that his ghost walk became ever more popular.

And so, every weekend (and alternate Wednesday evenings) for the last four years, Malcolm could be found in various pubs around the villages and towns, having garnered together a small group of interested people through his website, adverts in the local paper, and by general word-of-mouth. Most of these groups, it had to be said, consisted of holidaymakers rather than locals, who could presumably 'see' their ghosts any time they wanted to.

These outings inevitably started in a little village pub with a nice drink or two, to give them much-needed 'Dutch courage' for the ordeal ahead, and, on cold nights, to help them ward off the chill. This little ritual nearly always guaranteed that Malcolm's clients became very mellow and laid-back as the tour progressed. (Which would probably prove to be a great asset in the rare case that they actually 'saw' anything.)

They'd then proceed in an orderly file to numerous churches — always a good spot for paranormal activity — houses of various horrors, and other atmospheric places, with their host acting as guide.

In Malcolm's now considerable experience, often a good setting was worth far more than a 'near' ghost sighting, in terms of providing satisfaction for his clients, and one of his favourite walks involved a now defunct railway station, where overgrown tracks led off to bramble-filled fields. Here he had his punters standing on the deserted, overgrown platform, listening out for the ghostly chuff-chuff-chuff of an approaching steam engine that had crashed on the railway line back in 1898, with the loss of five lives.

Naturally, the ghost train had never yet had the temerity to actually show up, but his punters enjoyed the tale, standing in the moonlight (or better yet, fog) listening intently!

Another favourite spot was an old barn on a hill, where a dead tramp had been found, between the wars, and was rumoured to be heard snoring there on certain days of the year. Here, once, Malcolm and his small group had nearly had the stuffing scared out of them when, unknown to Malcolm, the farmer had moved his prize bull into the barn, and they'd definitely heard something big and heavy breathing under the dark rafters! Naturally, they'd all legged it pretty sharpish and had retired to the nearest hostelry, where the drinks had flowed faster than usual (his tips that night had been a record-breaker). Malcolm had only learned about the presence of the bull the next day, when he'd gone back in broad daylight and seen the placid animal for himself. But by then his punters, of course, had all dispersed to go about their normal lives, much enthused by their 'otherworldly' experience.

Not that he would have told anyone the true explanation anyway, even if he'd been able to track them down. For weeks after this incident — until the farmer moved his bull — that particular ghost walk had been very popular indeed, and his reputation as the man who could give someone a genuine ghostly experience had grown exponentially.

But now, as he propped up the bar of the Spindlewood Inn (one of his regular starting points), ruminating on his past glories was the last thing on his mind.

He'd known about the inn's Regency Extravaganza for a while, of course — Muriel and Richard had been pleased as punch to come up with such a good money-spinner right at the end of the summer tourist season.

Indeed, the local story of Hester and her ghost was on his regular tour of this area, and included a stop at the church to see her grave, and a walk past the big house where she'd once lived. So it was a no-brainer for him to choose this weekend to include the village of Caulcott Deeping in his walk. After all, he was bound to pick up some extra punters to add to his troop from the weekend guests at the inn.

But when he'd turned up with his group of nine (a slightly small group, to be sure, but then the tourist season was nearly over) he'd found a pub if not in mourning, then at least abuzz with gossip and nervous energy.

Which should have been a good thing — but now he wasn't so sure.

Malcolm's tours were very simply arranged. He'd give the designated meeting point on his website, always a pub, and after the initial drink or two, which gave time for any latecomers to turn up, they'd set off on their walk. Malcolm would then explain the 'ghost' they were trying to find and there'd be the usual mix of giggles and anxiety as they did their stuff. Then they'd all get back in their various cars (designated drivers having refrained from booze, naturally) and meet up at the next point on the walk, which would be another pub. And so the process was repeated until everyone had had enough ghost-hunting and they'd all go home.

And if the only spirits most of them ever saw were the spirits sold by the delighted pub landlords, nobody ever complained much. Although some 'dedicated' believers could be a bit bolshie over the non-appearance of an actual apparition. However, Malcolm only had to point out that ghosts, by their very nature, were bound to be capricious, and that he could hardly *guarantee* a sighting, and most would grudgingly concede that he had a point.

So when Malcolm had left the last pub nearly half an hour ago — which, as luck would have it, was in itself the 'haunted' building — and had told the story of Milton-in-the-Marsh's claim to ghostly fame, he'd mentioned the inn's weekend event and the am-dram re-enactment of the local legend. At the time, Malcolm had felt rather smug telling them all about it, as it had added an element of glamour to the usual experience. It wasn't often he could promise the chance to chat to glamorous luvvies, after all.

But for them to arrive and find that the actress playing Lady Hester had actually just died . . . well. Not to put too fine a point on it, it had rather put the dampeners on what had been shaping up to be a really convivial evening.

Mind you, he supposed morosely, as he stood sipping his second mild gin and tonic of the evening, in some ways it had certainly added a little piquancy to the proceedings. But he was a little wary about having such a potentially 'fresh' ghost to think about. Most of his starring players had been dead for many years — in some cases centuries. And the thought of being out and about in the dark merely hours after some poor girl had died . . .

Malcolm sighed heavily. He didn't like it. But he also wasn't sure just what he should do about it. Play it down? Play it up? Ignore it?

He eyed his latest group with a slightly jaundiced eye, trying to gauge their mood and what they might want to do now.

They were, by and large, a fairly representational bunch.

Over his many years in this business, Malcolm had come to learn that there were basically four types of punter.

By far his largest group of ghost-walkers consisted of tourists and holidaymakers, responding to the leaflets he left in various hotels, advertising a ghost walk in their area. These were very much of the 'why not have a bit of a laugh while we're here' variety, who tended on the whole to be good-natured, and enjoyed themselves hugely. Especially if a black cat shooting out of the bushes gave them a nice little turn just when Malcolm had got to a particularly scary part of his narration.

Then there were the kinda/wannabe believers, who came on the walk because their great-uncle Albert had sworn that he'd once seen his great-aunt Mabel's ghost in the coal shed or whatever. These, too, enjoyed the ghost stories, and were perhaps a little bit more spooked when tramping through a churchyard at night, but on the whole enjoyed the pub crawl as much as anything.

Then, less common than you might think, came the genuine, dedicated but 'amateur' believers who were convinced that they themselves had seen a ghost, or were desperate to see one. With these, Malcolm was very careful to pitch his stories with a bit less light-heartedness and drop in a bit more serious 'scholarly detail.'

And then, rarest of all (for which Malcolm was heartily glad) were what he thought of as the 'professional' ghost-hunters, who took things very seriously indeed. Thankfully, Malcolm didn't have to endure many of these, as they tended to regard ghost walks in general as being well beneath them.

Which was why, on this particular night, Malcolm was struggling to keep a happy smile on his face. Because news of the tragedy at the village pond had spread like wildfire, and Malcolm had just spotted two blokes in the crowd, laden down with various pieces of equipment, who were clearly intent on doing some very serious investigation indeed.

Malcolm, who recognised the infrared cameras and electronic equipment that was supposed to register 'ghostly voices or EVP' and 'magnetic emanations' and who-the-hell-knew-what-else, gazed at them with a jaundiced eye. People like these tended to talk your head off and bore you rigid — which was odd, since their subject matter should be so very interesting.

Which made him seriously contemplate cutting out the Caulcott Deeping walk altogether and going on somewhere else.

Unfortunately, not only had he already promised his group this walk, he could see now that they were all deep in animated conversation with the locals, who were only too willing to tell them all about the fatal afternoon that had just passed. And what else could be more fascinating than a tale of tragedy involving a beautiful young actress?

Even as he sipped his drink, he could hear an enthralled woman's voice talking to one of his punters. 'She was such a pretty thing. Who'd have thought she could die just from going into the pond? It was so unexpected. And the police have been here, talking to everyone!'

And, quick as a flash, a rather querulous voice that he recognised as belonging to a member of his group, shot back, 'Do you think it could be Lady Hester's revenge? Perhaps she didn't like it, this amateur theatre group doing her story? She might have taken offence! Perhaps she was waiting in the water and pulled this Rachel Norman woman down?'

The voice belonged to a seventy-something retired schoolteacher, who'd been boring the socks off the rest of them all evening, recounting his incident with a ghost when he'd been a boy. (Something to do with a woman in white at a bowling green. Or was it at a lawn tennis club?)

Now he sighed, and stood up a little straighter, and clapped his hands lightly. He couldn't let this sort of melodrama go unchecked. Before he knew it, things would be getting out of hand. 'Ladies and gentlemen of the McFadden Ghost Walk Tours,' he raised his voice effortlessly. 'As I can see you've already heard,' he began, when a short respectful silence had fallen, 'the village has suffered a very recent sad and tragic event. In light of this, I was wondering if you would prefer to skip this part of the tour and go straight on to Barton-on-the-Green instead?'

There was the usual frantic eye-catching that went on, as any group of only-just-met strangers tried to come to a consensus without actually speaking to one another. Eventually, the wife of a couple that were here on holiday from Scotland cleared her throat.

'Well, if it's all the same to you, I'd like to do the walk here.'

There was a vague general muttering that emphatically agreed with her. And Malcolm was no mug. Over the years he'd finely honed his ability to read his punters' moods, and he thought he had a pretty good measure of them now.

Ghouls, he thought with a bit of a sigh. All of them! 'Very well then. We can go to the church as planned, and then on to the house . . . Er, we will, of course, have to pass by the village pond on the way,' as if he didn't know that *that's* where they were all dying to go in order to have a good gawk! 'So, if anyone needs a stiff drink, I suggest you order one now, and we'll get on our way in . . . shall we say ten minutes?'

There was a brief rush to the bar, where Richard Sparkey was delightedly pushing his ruinously expensive brandy, and conversation broke out again in excited bursts and starts.

Over by her table near the window seat, Jenny Starling had listened to this exchange with a rather wry smile.

She remembered Muriel telling her about the scheduled ghost walk, and Min's eagerness to go on it. Now, she rather doubted that the American couple would be feeling so keen. In fact, as she looked around she couldn't see either of them. Perhaps they'd decided to have an early night.

She did catch the eye of Rory Gilchrist, however, who was looking at the gaggle of excited ghost-walkers with a rather sour smile of his own.

She herself wouldn't be caught dead going on the ghost walk. And then Jenny had to give an inner smile over her rather inapt choice of phrase.

Although none of the 'outsiders,' as she couldn't help but think of them, had known Rachel Norman, she couldn't help but think the whole thing was in rather bad taste. Clearly, nobody from the inn or the Regency Extravaganza were going to go.

But there, as it turned out, she was wrong.

For when the tour departed ten minutes later, Ion Dryfuss left his seat and went silently after them.

* * *

'So this is where the ex-fiancée hangs out,' Inspector Franklyn said. Felicity Thornton, like her one-time boyfriend, still lived in the family home, a semi-detached house remarkably similar to that of the Greenslades. Built around the same time but in a slightly larger and more run-down cul-de-sac,

Thomas Franklyn could sympathise with the youngsters' wish to get a place of their own. And for a moment, he felt vaguely sorry that the dead girl had come between them and ruined their dreams. Still, they were young and would doubtless get over it.

'What do we know about her?' he asked briskly, slamming the car door shut behind him and glancing around. A few rather pitiful streetlights had now come on, casting a rather sickly orange glow on the cracked pavements, but now that the unseasonably hot day had passed, a pleasantly cool evening breeze now stirred the leaves on the trees. Soon enough, he mused, that breeze would get colder as autumn finally arrived.

'She lives with her widowed mother, sir. No priors or previous,' Lucy rattled off. She glanced at her watch, seeing that it was nearly nine o'clock, and was glad that this was the last call of the day. She wanted to get off home and have a long soak in the bath, and watch an American TV programme she was addicted to on catch-up TV. Which, in Lucy's opinion, was the best invention since sliced bread.

'Right, best get on with it then,' Franklyn sighed. He, too, was sounding weary.

Mrs Thornton answered the door quickly, and then proceeded to look them up and down with a definite glint in her eye. Dressed in smart but casual tailored trousers and a lightweight sweater in a complicated knitted design, she had a chic jet-black geometric hairstyle and was wearing light make-up. In short, she looked like the sort of woman that you didn't argue with. Her mouth was pinched tight, and her grey eyes were narrowed slightly.

She reminded Lucy of one of her teachers back at school — one who'd always given her extra homework.

She reminded the inspector of a madam he'd once arrested back in the nineties, whose memory always managed to bring him out in a cold sweat.

'Mrs Thornton? Is your daughter, Felicity, in?' Franklyn got straight to the point.

'Why? Who are you?'

Both police officers hastily showed their identification.

'What do you want with my daughter?' she demanded. She had not, as yet, moved from her position squarely filling the doorway, and gave no indication that she was prepared to ask them in.

'We just have a few questions about her whereabouts this afternoon,' Franklyn said firmly. 'It's just routine,' he added.

What the dragon-lady might have said to this, luckily, they never got to learn, since a younger and far more friendly voice called over her shoulder, 'Mum, who is it?' and a moment later, a tall, raven-haired woman appeared. Her eyes were also grey, like her mother's, but they had a much more friendly look about them. Her expression, however, was puzzled. 'Who's this?' she asked.

'Police, Miss Thornton. We have just a few quick questions for you, if you don't mind,' the inspector said quickly, before her mother could speak.

'Me? You want to talk to me?' She sounded surprised, but gently reached out a hand and put it on her mother's shoulder. 'It's all right, Mum.' And to the police officers, 'Of course I don't mind. Do come on in,' she invited, and when her guardian dragon reluctantly moved to one side, they could see that she had a rather boyish figure, dressed in jeans and a pale green T-shirt.

'Would you like a cup of tea? Or coffee?' she offered.

'No, thank you,' Franklyn said. 'Although if you'd like to talk in the kitchen whilst you make yourself a cup, that would be fine,' he added quickly. In the hopes, of course, that her mother would take herself off to the lounge.

But Lucy could have told him that was a forlorn hope, and within five minutes all four of them were sitting down at the kitchen table, and Felicity — still with a rather puzzled frown on her face — set about answering their questions.

When she confirmed that she'd been around to Matthew Greenslade's house earlier, in order to call off their engagement and give him his ring back, Mrs Thornton's mouth pinched even tighter, but she remained mercifully silent.

'And when you left his house you came straight back here?' Franklyn asked.

'Yes,' Felicity agreed, looking between him and his sergeant. 'Why do you ask?'

'Was your mother here?' Franklyn asked, reluctantly turning his attention back to the elder Thornton.

'I was,' the lady said crisply, her tone of voice daring him to disbelieve her. Franklyn didn't. 'I work at the local council — in the planning office — and I was going through some applications. Sunday is supposed to be a day off, but it rarely is,' she said. 'I was working at my computer in the lounge and heard her come in. We ate dinner at about six. Lamb,' she added flatly.

'And you've been here all afternoon?' Franklyn said, turning once more to the daughter.

'Yes.' Felicity frowned, squirming a little on her seat. 'Look, is Matthew in trouble?'

'Fliss,' her mother said sharply. 'That boy is no longer your concern. Cheating on you like that. Forget about him,' she instructed.

Her daughter totally ignored her and kept her gaze on the inspector.

'Why do you ask?' Franklyn asked craftily.

Felicity sighed impatiently. 'Because you're here asking about him.'

'I'm actually asking about you, Miss Thornton,' Franklyn corrected her gently. 'Do you know the village of Caulcott Deeping?' he suddenly shot the question at her out of the blue.

Felicity blinked, but rallied quickly. 'Yes. It rings a bell . . . Wait a minute, that's where Matthew was doing some acting job this weekend. Something to do with a local historical re-enactment. He was nervous about having to try and ride a horse, or something.'

146

'Have you ever been there, Miss Thornton?' Franklyn persisted.

'I dunno,' the younger girl shrugged her shoulders. 'I must have done at some point, I suppose. I've always lived here,' she waved a hand around to encompass the town. 'I might have gone to the pub there at some point. It has a pub, right? That's where Matthew said he and the rest of the am-dram players were doing their gig.'

'Do you know Miss Rachel Norman — a player in his group?' Franklyn asked next, and beside him he felt the drag-on-lady stiffen angrily. She even let her breath out in a little hiss that made Lucy jump.

'His bit of stuff on the side you mean?' Mrs Thornton said angrily. 'What's she got to do with this?'

Her daughter's face, at the mention of the dead woman's name, clouded slightly, and she gave a brief nod. 'I've met her, yes. Once or twice, when I've gone to see Matthew's plays. They put on a pantomime for the school kids around Christmas time in the village halls. She played Dick Whittington, I think. So yes, we'd met. I can't say that I know her, though. Why?'

'She died this afternoon, whilst performing at Caulcott Deeping. It looks as if she may have drowned,' he added. Or not, he silently amended.

For a moment, both mother and daughter gaped at him, with identically stunned expressions.

'Oh,' Felicity finally said. And then, quietly, 'Does Matthew know?'

'He does now,' Franklyn said wryly. 'We've just come from Mr Greenslade's house.'

Felicity flushed. 'Does he . . . I mean, what did he say . . .'

'I can't reveal details about the investigation at this stage, Miss Thornton. I'm sure you can appreciate that,' Franklyn cut her off pompously.

'Felicity was here with me all this afternoon, from about three-thirty onwards, Inspector,' Mrs Thornton said quickly, perhaps sensing that her daughter was beginning to look a shade rebellious now. 'And as I've already said, that boy and his, er, companions, are no concern of ours. So, if that's all you needed to know . . . ?' And with that she stood up abruptly, making it very clear they were getting tossed out on their ears.

Franklyn, who didn't normally allow his witnesses to set the agenda, briefly debated being stubborn and refusing to go, but after a quick internal review, decided that there was little point. It was late, and he wanted to get home. And he didn't even know for sure yet whether or not he had a suspicious death on his hands. What's more, it was clear that wild horses wouldn't budge Mrs Thornton from providing an alibi for her daughter.

Always supposing she'd needed one.

'Thank you for your time,' the inspector said with an amiable smile at the younger woman, then nodded briskly at the older one, and followed his grateful sergeant out into the cooling night air.

Once safely walking down the garden path, Lucy O'Connor let out her breath in a whoosh.

'First thing in the morning, check around and see if any of our witnesses reported seeing a woman fitting Felicity's description at the scene. Or her mother's,' he added out of sheer spite. 'By then, we should have collated all the footage taken by the audience members on their mobile phones. See if you can spot her having been captured on film — or digital chip or whatever it's called nowadays.'

'Yes, sir,' Lucy said with a smile. 'And should I keep an eye out for Mrs Thornton too?'

'We should have the autopsy results and the preliminary forensics in first thing,' Franklyn said, blithely ignoring her cheek. 'Then at least we'll have a better idea of what's what. I know our superstar doc is starting work at sparrow fart,' he added, 'being so keen and eager to prove she didn't drown. Let's just hope that he finds evidence that she died of natural causes instead, and then we can pack the whole case in and just write up the reports.'

'Yes, sir,' Lucy agreed. But she had the feeling her superior wasn't holding out much hope for this particular scenario.

'We'll convene tomorrow at the Spindlewood Inn at nine o'clock sharp,' Franklyn said. 'I want to have another word with the Buckeys.'

He was also rather hoping the landlords at the inn would offer them breakfast on the house. He'd heard that Jenny Starling cooked like a dream.

* * *

Ion Dryfuss was feeling silly. It was nearly eleven o'clock at night, and he was standing in the dark, on the area of green in front of the pond, watching two men set up a small tent and lugging a large battery about as they set up various pieces of rather rickety-looking equipment.

The ghost walk had now ended, with Malcolm leading his group of curiosity-seekers onto another village in pursuit of a headless horseman or something, leaving behind an eerie silence, broken only by his companions. Occasionally one would mutter something about a camera playing up, and they seemed to be having trouble connecting a magnetic-energy-something-or-other to the battery.

He was left standing in the dark, staring at the pond and feeling . . . well . . . silly.

Here on the green there were no streetlights, although several of the cottages around had night-lights shining in their porches and through windows that had not yet had their curtains drawn. There was also a full moon, currently positioned behind the weeping willows on the far side of the pond, scattering pale, fragmented light.

His eyesight had long since become accustomed to the dark, and now he could see a surprising amount. Some water-fowl, unhappy with the activity on the bank, rustled restlessly about in the reeds.

'Did you bring the thermos of coffee?' one of the men asked his companion.

'Course I did,' his friend shot back, sounding annoyed.

Ion knew them only by the names of Mick and Steve, but they appeared to be oddly interchangeable, being the same height and build, and possessing the same untidy brown haircut. Both were dressed in jeans and loose-fitting rugby shirts. Both seemed to be young, barely out of their teens Ion suspected, and clearly thought of themselves as professional ghost-hunters. He suspected that they probably had part-time jobs at supermarkets, and were keen to find 'proof' of paranormal activity and get their own television programme on one of the digital channels that nobody ever watched.

Such was fame in the early twenty-first century.

They'd magnanimously allowed him to stay with them because of his previous relationship with the dead girl, and treated him — and his grief — with a mix of fascination and clumsy embarrassment.

When he'd first become aware of the ghost walk back at the inn, his first reaction had been one of almost hysterical laughter. He'd been sitting at the bar, feeling alternately numb and then cold with fear and rage and something else that he hadn't quite been able to give a name to.

So when Malcolm and his merry little group had arrived, seeking their ghostly encounters, he'd had to bite his lip hard to stop from laughing like a loon.

And he couldn't help but wonder what Rachel would have made of it all.

Then, as the laughter echoing around inside his head had slowly abated, he came to realise that Rachel would probably have thought it a hoot. And almost certainly would have joined in, had she been able to. And not just because she'd been game for a laugh either, but because she had possessed a surprisingly superstitious streak to her nature.

Ion was no fool. He knew even as he'd been falling for her back in Wales that she'd been hard-headed and ambitious, and had probably never genuinely felt love for anyone but herself in her life. And she'd made no bones about the fact that she'd always been able to see life for what it was: a dog-eat-dog world where you had to look out for number one. But for all her cynicism and grasp on reality, she'd also had a fey side — probably courtesy of her Irish grandmother. She'd liked to consult fortune tellers, for example, and had read her horoscope every day. And he wouldn't have been at all surprised to learn that she had believed in ghosts.

Was that why he'd tagged along when Malcolm's little group had eagerly trooped out the door? Had he, subconsciously, been hoping that if there *was* an afterlife, Rachel might come back — if only to say goodbye properly? Or even apologise for the way she'd treated him? Had he really lost his head to that extent?

Or had he, far more prosaically, simply not wanted to stay at the inn, knowing that everyone would be looking at him and wondering . . .

He didn't think that was the case either, not really. He'd simply wanted . . . what? To reconnect with Rachel somehow? If it was at all possible that her spirit, or shade, or essence, or aura, or whatever you wanted to call it, might still linger here in this place where she had died, was it really so wrong of him to want the chance to see for himself?

But the ghost walk had been pointless, and after the group had hung around the cordoned-off pond for a while — with, of course, nothing at all happening — they'd soon moved on to the next highlight of the tour.

Leaving only Ion and the two 'professional' ghost-hunters behind at the pond. The two lads, he knew, intended to spend the night here. Both were almost touchingly keen and eager to be on the spot so soon after a death. And in a way, their insensitive, youthful enthusiasm was like a balm to his ragged soul. They at least made no pretence to be anything other than keen as mustard to revel in the experience.

Here, if Ion could only appreciate it, was evidence that life went on as normal — whatever normal was. That here, in these silly, excited, happy lads, was proof that he could survive without her.

So as the night gradually wore on, and the cottage lights around him were turned off, one by one, Ion stayed, a silent witness on the green, his eyes drifting restlessly over the pond.

Mick — or was it Steve? — was trying to set up an arc light with a slightly reddish glow to it, but the battery they'd brought didn't seem to want to do the job and it kept flickering. With much cursing, they'd finally disassembled it and put it away.

Now one of them yawned over his audio equipment, whilst another sat on a folding stool, staring at the screen on his laptop. Ion, who'd looked at it once over the lad's shoulder, had seen only a representation of a graph. Catching him watching, Steve — or was it Mick? — had explained that it was recording electro-magnetic energy. He was a bit miffed at all the 'interference' from the village around him though, and the overhead power lines. But he assured Ion that should a ghost put in an appearance, the readings would 'go wild.'

So far, they hadn't gone wild.

Behind him, Ion Dryfuss heard the village church clock strike midnight. Traditionally the witching hour, he thought with a sardonic grin. And at the sound, the two lads became very still and excited. But nothing moved — not even a local cat, out on the prowl. Nothing ruffled the calm waters of the pond, no footsteps could be heard echoing around the green, nor in the air around them.

Midnight passed.

And about half an hour later, Ion wondered how much longer he was going to stand in the dark, by the pond, waiting for Rachel to . . . what?

Over in the woods beyond the farmer's field, Ion heard a tawny owl call out.

He was about to give up, turn away and go back to his room at the inn.

And then Ion saw something.

CHAPTER ELEVEN

At first, he wasn't sure. He just caught a sense of movement out of the corner of his eye, and even then, when he turned to look more closely, he was almost inclined to believe it was a trick of the moonlight and shadow and was about to look away again.

But then he heard a faint but definite rustle and he turned back sharply to look once more, his eyes fixed to the side of the pond where the bull rushes grew the thickest. Perhaps it was just some wildlife after all.

And then a dense dark shape moved, and suddenly he was sure beyond all doubt. That was no fox or trick of the light. Something dark and very definitely human-shaped was moving out there, by the pond.

Instantly, he felt his heart rate leap as a lance of pure, primeval fear shot up his spine, leaving him cold and trembling. And for a moment he felt a wave of nausea sweep over him so intense that he felt as if he might actually be sick. Was it possible Rachel *had* come back to haunt him?

Swallowing hard he took a stumbling step forward, his eyes straining to make out exactly *what* it was he was seeing. At the same time he half whispered and half croaked harshly, 'Lads! Lads, I can see something.' Right now, even the company of some callow youths was better than being alone in the night with his fear.

Not surprisingly, both lads were by his side in an instant, and Ion could almost feel their excitement, it was so palpable. 'What? Where?' one of them hissed back.

Wordlessly, Ion pointed at the pond. Then, feeling stupid, managed to be a bit more specific. 'Just this side, near where Rachel went in, but in the bull rushes growing next to her entry point.'

'OK. What exactly did you see?' the other one asked eagerly. 'A mist, a white shape, a glowing orb floating in the air — what?'

'A dark shape — a human shape,' Ion said.

'Sure it wasn't just a shadow?' he asked, sounding a bit disappointed now. 'The moonlight's quite bright, and with all the trees around, a breeze moving the leaves can make you think you see movement where there isn't any.'

Ion shrugged. Now he wasn't so sure. And now nothing seemed to be moving. Nevertheless, he didn't believe his eyes had been playing tricks. 'It was definitely a dark mass and it was person-shaped. It wasn't dappled moonlight,' he said firmly.

'Mick, you got the thermal imaging glasses?' Steve hissed impatiently, and Mick quickly held up a pair of what, to Ion, looked like a virtual-reality headset. A sort of cross between a frogman's diving mask and a pair of wraparound flat binoculars.

Both lads slipped them on, and then went very still.

'Oh shit,' one lad finally said. His voice was a bit wavering and Ion could sense a different kind of tension in the air now.

Ion, who thought it had passed, felt his nausea return with a vengeance. 'What? What is it?' he asked urgently, his mouth and tongue feeling so dry he could hardly form the words. He wished they'd brought a third pair with them so that he could see what they were seeing. 'Is it a ghost?' His granny, whose own mother had been said to 'have the sight' had told him that he was a little fey. Now he wondered if that was true and if that was why Rachel's spirit had homed in on him.

'Nah, don't think so. What do you say, Steve?' the lad standing nearest him whispered, his prosaic words thankfully dampening Ion's fevered imagination somewhat.

'Nah. It's nothing supernatural,' the other lad whispered back. 'You got your mobile, mate?'

'Sure. Who'd you want me to call?' Mick fumbled a hand into one of his pockets and withdrew his phone. 'The cops, you reckon?'

'Yeah, I reckon,' his friend said nervously.

By now, Ion was almost shifting from foot to foot with impatience. 'What's going on? *What is it?* Did I see something?' he hissed.

'Yeah,' Steve said quietly, sounding distinctly jittery now. 'There's someone hunkered down in those bull rushes. And they're watching us.'

Ion swallowed hard. 'How do you know? All I can see is a dark patch.'

'Thermal imaging shows body heat,' he explained, as his mate keyed in 999 on his mobile. To Ion, the tiny beep, beep, beep it made as he did so sounded incredibly loud in the still night air. But then, he was standing right next to the phone — surely whoever it was who was creeping about out there hadn't heard it?

But could whoever it was hear them whispering? Well, if so, what did it matter? They clearly knew that Ion and the others were here — if they were watching them from the cover of the bull rushes.

And the fear that had turned Ion's spine to ice shifted slightly and became something far more familiar, and in a strange way, more welcome. Gone was the panic-inducing paranoia of the unknown, and in its stead came a more steely, fight-or-flight response. Now that he knew he was dealing with a potentially malevolent but *human* threat, he felt better able to cope.

Not that Ion had ever been in a real fight, but at least if whoever it was out there attacked, he knew he wouldn't be dealing with the supernatural.

'Body heat means that it's an animal or something living, so of no use to us,' the other lad continued to explain nervously, even as these thoughts flitted in and out of Ion's head. 'Ghosts don't have heat — in fact, they produce cold spots.'

'Are you sure it's not a fox or something?' Ion whispered hopefully.

'Nah — wrong shape, mate,' this hope was quickly shot down in flames. 'You go out at night as often as we do, you quickly get to spot foxes, deer, owls in flight, badgers, rabbits, you name it. This is definitely a person, like you said — they're hunkered down, but I can make out a face, and hands. And whoever he is, he's interested in us, cause he's staring right this way.'

'Oh shit,' Ion said. And then wondered — shouldn't he be doing something? Something other than standing here like a petrified pillock? Because if Rachel hadn't died of natural causes — and he was no mug, he could tell that the cops weren't satisfied about something — then what if that was her killer out there?

Shouldn't he be brave and confront him? Nab him and sit on him until the cops came?

'Yeah, police. It's urgent.' The lad on the phone had obviously just got through to the emergency switchboard. 'Look, mate, I'm over at Caulcott Deeping, where that girl died this afternoon, and there's someone messing about with the crime scene! Oh hell, he's taking off — you need to get someone over here quick!'

His voice rose in panic and excitement as he spoke, and even without the aid of the night-vision glasses, Ion could see for himself that the dark figure was now moving around the pond — and wasn't going to any particular pains to try and hide it, either. In fact, he, she or it was bolting from the edge of the pond and heading towards the far side where it was fenced off from the farmer's field.

Just a dense black shape against a slightly less black background, Ion couldn't get a sense of whether he was looking at a fat man, a thin woman, a teenager or someone older.

And then instinct kicked in as Ion, with a shout of general outrage, shot off after it. He wasn't sure whether the sight of the fleeing figure had triggered some atavistic hunting instinct in him, or whether his subconscious was telling him that he had nothing to fear from a fleeing predator. He only knew that white-hot anger and a vicious desire to get his hands on whoever it was out there had now replaced his fear.

Unfortunately, the fast-moving dark shape had a long head start on him, and even as he ignored the two lads shouting warnings for him to 'leave it' and 'don't be so bloody daft!' he doubted that he'd be able to make up the lost ground.

That didn't stop him from trying though, and he cut across the green at a reckless pace given that he couldn't even see where he was putting his feet, and belted headlong for the footpath that circumnavigated the pond. As he reached it though, in the dark, he failed to see that there was a slight but definite decline down onto the path and his forward motion made him stumble and nearly take a header into the pond, careening through the police tape. He managed to right himself just in time by windmilling his arms, only to look up and see the fleeing figure haul itself neatly up and over the chain-link fence and disappear into the moonlit expanse of the meadow beyond.

Even as he watched, the figure gained further ground and disappeared into the night.

'Shit!' Ion gasped again, panting in a mixture of disappointment, defiance and rage. He was rather touched, a moment later, to sense that both lads had joined him, and had come up on either side of him, both of them panting hard. Although they might not have agreed with the chase, they hadn't wanted to leave him to it and perhaps face the threat on his own. Either that, or their own sense of machismo wouldn't let them stay behind. Teenage boys weren't known for their good sense, after all.

'Legged it, has he?' Mick (or was it Steve) asked, trying — and to his credit, mostly succeeding — in sounding nonchalant and rather matter-of-fact.

'Yeah. Are the cops coming?' Ion asked miserably.

'Yep. They told us to stay put. So I reckon we'd better get back to the tent.'

Ion sighed and nodded and trudged back after them. He was rather surprised that Inspector Franklyn hadn't left a copper on duty at the pond. But then he supposed, given the government cutbacks and lack of funding, he hadn't been able to spare the resources to do so. The police tape should've been enough to warn normal folk to keep away.

And the Welshman wouldn't have been human if he hadn't felt a little smug that no doubt the senior policeman would soon be regretting his lack of foresight.

Then his sense of satisfaction fled as a bone-aching weariness set in. No doubt the cops would want to have chapter and verse on what had just happened. And the fact that Ion had been here in the middle of the night would make them look at him with even more suspicion than they had before.

No. He wasn't expecting his second police interview to go any better than the first.

* * *

Jenny Starling was setting aside freshly laid eggs in order to make some breakfast omelettes, when she first heard about the excitement in the night.

'Bloody young fool! He should have had more sense,' she heard Muriel say as she came through the kitchen door. She was talking over her shoulder to her husband, who had been helping her lay the tables in the dining room.

'Who should?' she asked cheerfully as her employers walked into the kitchen and stopped dead in their tracks to look at her in surprise. At only six in the morning, they were probably surprised to find her already up and about.

'Oh, our young Welsh friend,' Muriel said vaguely, with a brief wave of her hand. 'I think some guests might be eating early this morning, Jenny,' she informed, abruptly changing the subject.

'No problem,' Jenny assured her professionally.

And during the next hour, as the dining room slowly filled up and Ion came down and told everyone about what had happened in the night, the gossip and excitement of that began to filter through to Jenny in the kitchen. And the more she learned all about it, the less she liked it.

Because why would someone be interested in the pond now? Oh, she knew all about that hoary old chestnut that stated that a killer always felt compelled to return to the scene of his or her crime, but like all sane people, didn't give it much credence. It might have been true in Victorian melodramas, but modern-day criminals had far more sense than to risk getting nabbed by doing something so daft.

So why had someone waited until gone midnight and then searched the area? Idle curiosity just didn't cover it. No. Somebody must have had an urgent need to check on something specific, or to search for something vital, maybe? Had something gone wrong with the plan, had a mistake been made that needed to be rectified?

Frowning, Jenny made sure that the bacon for her traditional English breakfast wasn't burning under the grill — it wasn't — and reached for her phone. Quickly, she searched for the telephone number Inspector Franklyn had left for her, and hit the call button.

She didn't know what his plans were for the day, and hoped that he wasn't still in bed. Something told her that Inspector Franklyn was the sort of man who'd be grumpy and snappish if roused from a sound sleep.

But she was doubly lucky. Not only was Franklyn already up, but both he and his sergeant were planning to meet at the inn. And the inspector was only too happy to accept her offer of breakfast for him and his junior officer, on the house.

159

Jenny didn't know what Richard or Muriel would have to say about this promise of free food, but she didn't think that even the money-grubbing Sparkeys would have the nerve to present the police officers with a bill!

As Muriel had predicted, most of the Regency weekenders were early risers that morning as well — probably because most of them had slept poorly. Also, none of them seemed to have much of an appetite, to Jenny's genuine dismay and distress, and most of them opted for cereal and toast, and only picked at these. Jenny tried not to take it personally.

On the plus side, it did mean that by the time the police officers arrived, the dining room had been used and cleared and was once again empty, so Jenny was able to provide a nice spread for them — and herself — on a cleared table by the window. And they could talk without being overheard.

Franklyn eyed the spread of omelettes, French toast, beautifully browned sausages and crispy bacon with an eager eye.

'Thanks for this,' he said with a happy sigh, pulling out his chair and stuffing his napkin into the front of his shirt. 'I was wanting to have a word with you anyway,' he began, the moment he'd sat down and speared a sausage. Jenny poured them a cup of coffee each and topped up her own cup.

'Good — I wanted to speak to you too. Have you heard about Ion's adventures at the pond last night?' she interrupted him, rather rudely, but she needed to make sure that he'd understood the full urgency of the matter and had taken the proper steps.

Franklyn gave a brief nod. 'The night-duty officer made a report and phoned me first thing.'

'I hope you made sure someone stayed on duty all night at the pond?' Jenny said, helping herself to a slice of French toast and taking a bite. Good. Hot and savoury, just how it should be (Worcestershire sauce was one of the greatest inventions of mankind, in her book).

'Don't try and teach your grandmother to suck eggs,' Franklyn told her off grumpily. 'Of course I had a young

160

constable stay there until . . .' he checked his watch, 'the divers get there. Which should be in about twenty minutes from now.'

Opposite her, Lucy O'Connor took a bite of the lightly herbed omelette and briefly closed her eyes in bliss. She'd never been able to get the hang of a good omelette herself — they either turned out to have the consistency of rubber, or the eggs were raw and runny in the middle. But this was perfect.

'Any idea what matey-boy was after last night?' Franklyn asked the cook curiously. He seemed unconscious of the fact that he was now treating her like a member of his team, and his sergeant hid her smile with another bite of the deliciously light and fluffy omelette.

Jenny shrugged, then frowned. Thinking back to yesterday afternoon, one particular episode did spring to mind . . . Was it possible . . . ? She opened her mouth to say something, but at that moment Franklyn held up a finger.

'Oh, before I forget, we've got the preliminary forensic reports in. About that air rifle,' he began portentously. 'It was wiped clean — no prints on it at all. Which is rather significant, don't you think?' he asked, eyes twinkling. Although his policeman's mind had instantly recognised the fact that no fingerprints meant that it couldn't have belonged to some innocent local, he wondered how long it would take the cook to realise the same thing.

Jenny blinked then beamed at him. 'Oh good! I'm so glad!'

Franklyn paused, and the piece of sausage that was halfway to his mouth hovered in mid-air. Beside him, Lucy too shot Jenny a quick, puzzled look.

'You are?' the inspector said blankly. He had no idea why this particular piece of news should please the cook so much. Although the presence of the wiped-clean air rifle now made it a significant item — somehow — in what had happened yesterday, it didn't exactly fill him with such good cheer.

'Oh yes!' Jenny enthused. 'I really do *like* Min and Silas, you see, and so I'm very glad that they're now in the clear. And I know you had to suspect them of creating that diversion on purpose.'

Franklyn blinked, his mind a total blank. 'Oh, er, right,' he said, and slowly proceeded to chew his sausage thoroughly. And since it wasn't polite to talk with your mouth full, he made a great show of his mastication. His mind, however, began to race. Damn it, what had this damned irritating woman seen so instantly that he hadn't?

Jenny beamed at his agreement and attacked her slice of French toast with renewed vigour. Like she'd just said, she'd never really liked to believe that the American couple had been involved, and hearing Franklyn give them the all-clear had made her day. 'So what else have you got?' she asked cheerfully.

Luckily, it was Lucy O'Connor who came to her boss's rescue. 'Sorry, I don't get why you think the American couple are now out of it,' she said, thus saving Franklyn from the ignominy of being forced to ask the question himself.

Jenny, hastily chewing the remains of a mouthful of French toast, swallowed hard. 'Well, because there were no fingerprints on the rifle,' she repeated. Jenny looked from Franklyn, still hastily and innocently chewing his breakfast, and then back to Lucy's frowning face, a little frown of worry appearing on her own forehead.

'So?' the blonde-haired young woman asked, a shade impatiently.

Jenny took a sip of coffee. Did the sergeant not agree with Franklyn and her own assessment as to where the evidence was clearly pointing? 'So clearly the rifle had been left there by the killer,' Jenny said, nodding her head happily, 'and not by some random villager.'

Lucy sighed. 'I get *that*,' the young blonde woman said testily. 'What I *don't* get is why that should let Min and Silas Buckey off the hook,' she persisted.

'Oh,' Jenny said, a shade blankly. 'But it's obvious, isn't it?' But it clearly wasn't obvious to Lucy, who was still staring back at her with a mixture of growing anger and bafflement.

'What was the rifle there for?' Jenny asked kindly, trying to help her out.

Franklyn speared another sausage and cast his sergeant a sympathetic look. He wasn't following the cook's reasoning any more than she was, but he was happy to sit back and see where this all went — because he would have bet a month's salary that Jenny Starling was about to pull one of her famous rabbits from the hat.

'We don't know,' Lucy said, beginning to sound aggrieved now.

'But what does a rifle do?' Jenny persisted patiently.

'It shoots things,' Lucy snapped.

'Exactly! In other words, it makes a damned big awful racket. A big bang, a sharp noise — something that simply can't be ignored by anyone who hears it, especially if it's fired at close quarters to you.'

'A distraction!' Franklyn suddenly yelped, almost spraying the tablecloth with masticated sausage in his sudden excitement. Because now he'd finally got it, at last — he'd twigged what the exasperating cook was getting at! 'If Min hadn't made a fuss about the spider, someone could have fired off the rifle and made everyone look away from the pond in that way!' he explained to his sergeant.

'Exactly,' Jenny said, nodding happily. 'And the presence of that rifle always *did* have the feel of a Plan B about it, don't you think?' She gave the two police officers a grin. 'You know, a sort of backup in case of emergency.'

'Which means,' Franklyn pressed on, desperate to get it out before Jenny could pip him to the post, 'that the killer deliberately put the spider on Min Buckey's shoulder, hoping that she'd do exactly what she did do, and get everyone's attention trained on her. But if she didn't spot the spider, or it simply fell off before she could see it — well, the rifle could be fired as an alternative distraction.'

'Which means that Min was used by the killer, and thus couldn't have had anything to do with it,' Jenny nodded. 'If Min or Silas *had* been in on whatever it was that happened to Rachel, there wouldn't have been any need for a Plan B would there? The rifle wouldn't have been needed.'

Lucy, looking a little chagrined, conceded rather reluctantly that the cook's logic seemed sound. And her respect for her boss went up a notch or two. Franklyn might have the reputation back at the station house for being a bit old-school, but there were clearly no flies on him.

'Mind you,' Franklyn said now morosely, 'until the quacks are finished doing the autopsy — which with any luck should be any time now — we don't even know if there is a "killer" involved at all. Although,' he added quickly, as both women looked at him sharply, 'clearly there's something underhanded going on here.'

'I'd say so,' Lucy began, but just then Franklyn's mobile went, and he reached into his jacket pocket and lifted it out. 'DI Franklyn,' he said crisply. He listened for a moment, frowned, and glanced at his watch. 'Hmmm. Funny that — I would have said that he was the type to be a stickler about time. You know what solicitors are like — time is money. Don't worry, he'll probably show up sooner or later. Has our super-doc nearly finished his post-mortem examination do you know?' He paused, sighed, then said, 'Right. But make sure he calls me the moment he's finished. I don't want to have to wait for his written report.' And then he hung up.

He hastily took a last bite of sausage and nodded across to his sergeant. 'It seems Mr Braine, our local friendly neighbourhood solicitor, hasn't turned up for his appointment at the police station. We'd better go and see what's keeping him.' He rose and then glanced down at Jenny kindly. 'Thanks for the breakfast — it was superb.'

Jenny, rather distractedly, smiled back at him. 'Don't mention it,' she murmured vaguely. And watched him go with rather troubled eyes.

She didn't like the sound of Vince Braine's no-show at the police station.

She didn't like the sound of Ion's adventures last night either.

And something was telling her that she was being very dim indeed about this whole affair. Something, she was sure, was staring her in the face and she just wasn't seeing it . . .

CHAPTER TWELVE

Dr Rory Gilchrist was hastily packing his cases. He wore a vaguely disgruntled expression, and cursed a bit under his breath as a recalcitrant sweater refused to fit into the space he'd left for it without creasing the shirt underneath. With a sigh, he shoved it down anyway.

No two ways about it, the Regency Extravaganza had turned out to be a total disaster, and he was looking forward to getting back to his college. With a bit of luck, after a decent tea, even the dull chat that could be expected at High Table would act like a perfect panacea for his frazzled nerves.

He glanced at his watch. Nearly ten-thirty. Perfect. A quick soft drink in the bar, and then he'd set off and should be back in Oxford by twelve at the latest — traffic and road conditions permitting.

In that, however, Dr Gilchrist was being unduly optimistic.

* * *

Jenny Starling was in the kitchen putting the finishing touches to her quiche Lorraine, which was making up part of the lunchtime menu, when she just caught a glimpse of

166

Inspector Franklyn going past the bar and heading up the stairs but wasn't in time to stop him.

For whilst the police had been absent, Jenny had been doing a lot of thinking — about stray corsets, torn reticules, Rachel Norman's love of money, and a lot more besides. And if the conclusions she was coming to proved to be correct . . .

Grimly, she took off her apron, popped her quiches in the oven to cook, then scrupulously washed her hands at the sink. She still had some pea and ham soup to prepare, but right now she had something even more pressing to do.

Like it or not — and Jenny most definitely did not — it was time she had a quiet word or two with the inspector.

* * *

Jenny was sitting in her favourite window seat, waiting for the inspector to come back downstairs. She was not looking forward to the upcoming interview one little bit.

But she didn't think she'd got things wrong. In fact, no matter how hard she tried to rearrange the facts, or pick holes in her thinking, she was pretty sure that the murder of Rachel Norman could only have happened in one way. And knowing *how* it was done firmly pointed the finger at *who* must have done it. The only thing she wasn't totally sure of was the motive — but she was confident a quick trawl of the police records would quickly establish that.

As the travelling cook sat in the sunshine streaming in through the open window and morosely contemplated the intricacies of a young girl's death, Sergeant Lucy O'Connor pushed open the door to the inn and stepped inside. Since it was barely past opening time, the only customer was Old Walter, who was sitting in his favourite stool by the bar sipping his beer. Richard Sparkey had left the bar empty, and had gone back into the kitchen, probably in search of a snack before he could expect the onslaught of the lunchtime crowd.

The sergeant looked around the empty room, glanced at Jenny, and was about to go past her, no doubt to head upstairs where she expected to find her superior officer questioning Rory Gilchrist, when the inspector stepped out from the door behind the bar.

He spotted his sergeant immediately and began to walk briskly towards her. They had found the solicitor at home with car trouble. He had given his statement, and had somewhat reluctantly confirmed that the Oxford academic had been having 'trouble' with his ex-wife. But although Gilchrist had just confirmed this, he couldn't see how it could possibly give him a motive to want Rachel dead.

He had a slight scowl and he briefly shook his head at the younger woman's questioning gaze. As he did so, his phone began to vibrate and he pulled it impatiently out of his pocket.

'Bloody hell!' he said. 'We've got the results of the autopsy in at last. And you're not going to believe this!'

Lucy blinked. 'What? Don't tell me it was natural causes after all?' she asked, her head spinning.

'No,' Franklyn said, his face darkening. 'She was murdered all right. And not only that — we know now who must have killed her!'

'We do?' Lucy said with delight, as Jenny Starling sat up a little straighter in her chair, a look of relief crossing her own face at the thought that perhaps she might not have to have that awkward little chat with the inspector after all.

'Yes, we do,' Inspector Franklyn reiterated. 'In fact, given this new information, there's only one person who could possibly have done it! Sergeant, you have your cuffs with you?'

'Yes, sir,' Lucy said smartly, reaching for the handcuffs on her belt. Her heart was beating faster in a mixture of excitement, triumph and dread. For the first time in her career she was actually going to arrest a murderer! Now this was what she'd joined the police service for!

'OK then. Let's go. You can also read him his rights if you like. Don't mess it up.'

'Thanks, sir, but who is it?' Lucy all but shouted.

'Ion Dryfuss,' Franklyn said flatly.

And Jenny Starling's heart sank.

Before they could leave, she stood up abruptly. 'Excuse me, Inspector, but I really don't think that's a good idea,' she said. She didn't shout — in fact, she doubted that her voice carried even so far as Old Walter sitting by the bar. But her quiet words jerked both police officers to a halt.

Quickly, Franklyn looked over at her and scowled. 'I'll ask you not to interfere, Miss Starling,' he said firmly. 'I won't deny you've been helpful so far, mind, but . . .'

'Inspector, I'm sorry, but . . .' Jenny wanted to tell him that if he arrested the Welshman now he'd only look foolish when he was forced to release him again later, but she wasn't quite sure how to put this tactfully. Instead, she decided to come at things from a different angle.

'Can you tell me why you think only Ion could have killed Miss Norman?' she asked instead. 'It'll only take a few moments, and I really do think I might be able to help.'

Franklyn was about to tell her, rather pithily, that he wasn't in the habit of sharing police information with members of the public, but then he caught Lucy's pleading eye, and realised that his sergeant, too, was still in the dark. After a quick glance around, confirming that there was no one in a position to overhear them, he moved a little closer, and bent his head.

And with Lucy listening in on one side of him and Jenny on the other, he quietly told them what the pathologist had discovered.

'Rachel Norman didn't drown. She was suffocated,' he said flatly. 'Some faint bruising, which only became apparent hours after her death, showed that someone had held a hand over her mouth and nose and suffocated her.'

'Bloody hell,' Lucy breathed.

'Exactly,' Franklyn nodded. 'And the only person who could have done that is the person who pretended to drag her out of the pond, but in fact actually took the opportunity to kill her instead. Ion Dryfuss.'

'Oh but that can't be right, sir!' Lucy said aghast, and at the exact same moment, Jenny Starling too shook her head, and said, 'No, I'm afraid that won't wash.'

The two women both broke off and looked at each other questioningly, and Inspector Thomas Franklyn felt his heart sink. It was, of course, to his sergeant that he turned first.

'What do you mean?' he demanded. 'Why can't it have been Dryfuss?'

But instead of explaining herself, Lucy fumbled with her mobile phone, tapped at it for a bit, and then handed it over to the inspector. 'I downloaded all the images taken that day by members of the public. And see this one here . . . it's really clear . . .'

Franklyn looked at the tiny screen on the phone, and watched as Ion Dryfuss leapt into the pond and waded out towards Rachel's body. Where he took her by *one arm* and then pulled her floating form towards him. He then turned her over onto her back, and with one arm under her, and the other arm in full view as he used it to help him propel towards the shore, towed her after him.

'You can see for yourself, sir,' Lucy said helplessly. 'He never put a hand anywhere near her face, let alone over her nose and mouth.'

'But then . . .' Franklyn gaped at Lucy, feeling totally at a loss, 'how the *hell* did he manage to smother her?'

'He didn't,' Jenny Starling said flatly. 'But if you'll sit down for a minute, I'll tell you who I think did.'

CHAPTER THIRTEEN

For a second the two police officers simply stared at Jenny, then they shot a quick, questioning glance at each other. Franklyn looked rueful and gave a brief sigh. He'd been warned about moments like this from other coppers who'd had the questionable pleasure of working with this woman. Now it looked like it was his turn to be amazed, so he reached out and pulled up a chair at her table. Lucy O'Connor quickly followed suit.

Jenny cast a quick glance around, but the bar was still totally deserted, save for Old Walter who was busily and happily completing a crossword puzzle in the local newspaper.

'OK. Where do you want to start?' Jenny asked quietly.

'How,' Inspector Franklyn said at once. 'I just can't get my head around how she was killed. She was smothered, for Pete's sake, and the only person who was in a position to do it — Dryfuss — quite clearly didn't do it.'

'Well, that's the easiest part,' Jenny said with a sigh. 'And when you think about it logically, it's rather obvious.' Luckily she didn't see the flash of annoyance that crossed Franklyn's resentful face as she said this, since she was frowning down thoughtfully at a beer mat in front of her on the table. 'If Rachel Norman couldn't possibly have been smothered after she walked into the pond, then it follows that she must have been smothered before she did so. Right?'

Lucy O'Connor blinked. 'Huh?'

Jenny raised her head and smiled grimly. 'Rachel Norman didn't die at the pond, Sergeant. She quite literally couldn't have. No, I think she must have died right here, at the inn,' she said quietly. 'Upstairs in the changing room, I imagine.'

Now Franklyn and his sergeant swapped wary glances. Clearly, both were wondering if the fabled cook had finally flipped her lid.

'But you saw her come down and do her act,' Lucy objected. 'You followed her to the pond, as did all the others, and watched her go into the water.'

'No we didn't,' Jenny said flatly. 'We watched *someone* come downstairs, dressed in full costume with a thick veil over her face, give a performance, walk down to the pond, and wade out into the middle. It just wasn't Rachel Norman. She was already dead by then.'

'Bloody hell,' Franklyn breathed. 'That would work! In fact, that would make sense of the pathologist's report. So . . . it must have been a woman who killed her? And took her place?'

'Wait a minute though,' Lucy again objected. 'Didn't you hear her speak? The actress I mean? All along I've been hearing how she had this magnificent sexy voice. The killer must have been one hell of a mimic to act out that whole scene in a fake voice! And I just don't know that I can swallow that.'

'Nor should you,' Jenny agreed, making Lucy's mouth drop open in surprise. 'I doubt that even the best professional impersonator or television star could have copied Rachel's voice so accurately and for so long. No, it was Rachel's voice we heard all right — there was no mistaking it, believe me. But it wasn't her "live" voice that we were hearing, but a recording. Do you remember, I told you about Rachel recording her rehearsal performances on a state-of-the-art digital recorder thing?'

Franklyn snapped his fingers. 'Of course! The killer must have found that final scene of Rachel's all rehearsed and recorded and simply used that.'

'Exactly. All she needed to do was turn it on at the right moment and then just slip the gizmo inside her reticule — the little fancy bag,' Jenny clarified at the inspector's puzzled look, 'which she wore on her arm. It was recovered from the edge of the pond later. You must have it in your evidence bags somewhere,' Jenny said.

'At the time, I remember seeing the bag by the edge of the pond, and noticed that it had a hole in it,' she swept on. 'At the time I assumed that it must have been damaged when it was dropped into the pond but even then I thought the slit in it looked rather neat and clean for a random tear. Now of course, it makes sense.'

'The killer needed to make a hole in it, so that the recorded voice wouldn't sound muffled,' Franklyn put in excitedly, catching on instantly.

'Exactly,' Jenny said. 'It was very clever since the voice came out clear as a bell, and because it was so distinctive, none of us watching ever questioned that it was Rachel. In that the killer was probably helped because, well, frankly, Rachel wasn't really the best actress you'd ever seen. Apart from her voice, which was wonderful. So any awkwardness or lack of professionalism in the performance . . . well, let's just say that we wouldn't have wondered about it. Unfortunately for the killer though,' Jenny swept on, 'later on, that same digital recorder became something of a liability, because when the impostor stepped into the pond she almost slipped and the reticule fell off her arm, dumping the evidence — the recorder — into the water. Of course, the original plan was to keep it and destroy it as soon as possible.'

'That's why it had to be recovered later,' Lucy jumped in eagerly. '*That's* what Ion and those ghost-hunter blokes saw and interrupted last night. Someone trying to recover the recorder before we did.'

'Because they knew the divers were due to come the next day — this morning — and search the pond,' Franklyn put in, glancing at his watch. 'They should be there now in fact. They'd better bloody find it,' he added darkly.

Jenny nodded reassuringly. 'I'm sure they will. The gadget would have been small but heavy and would have sunk straight to the bottom — and it was right by where she went in. You might like to ask them to concentrate on that area first, by the bull rushes.'

She waited whilst Franklyn made the call, and as he did so, she could see Lucy O'Connor's mind was racing.

The moment he hung up, Lucy asked her next question. 'But how did the killer arrange for the distraction with Min and the spider when she was already in the pond?'

'She didn't,' Jenny said flatly. 'She couldn't, could she? No, it was her accomplice who did that.'

'There were two of them,' Franklyn said, sounding faintly surprised. Murders with more than one perpetrator were quite rare, in his experience.

'Oh yes,' Jenny sighed. 'When you think of it, it would have to take two. One to kill Rachel, and then transport her body in the back of a car or van to the far side of the pond and place her in the water, in the only spot where you *could* hide a body. Hidden under that little jetty,' she added quickly, as both police officers frowned over that. 'He'd only have had to secure her loosely to the wooden timbers so that she didn't float free, and be ready for later on. Don't forget, at the back of the pond there's that line of weeping willow trees, with the fronds reaching right down to the water, providing him with the perfect cover, if any villager should have been out and about and walking past. All he then had to do was get out and change into his dry costume and mingle with the crowds, wait for his accomplice to arrive, and at the right moment, put the spider, probably kept in a matchbox or something, on Min's shoulder. Again, he'd be — to all intents and purposes — in disguise, like a lot of people there. So even if anybody did notice him close to Min, they'd be looking more at his outfit than at his face. Therefore if he was spotted actually putting the spider on her shoulder, he had a good chance of not being recognised. And, as we already know, if the spider trick didn't work, he had the rifle as a backup plan to make everyone turn away for those precious few minutes.'

'And in those few minutes,' Franklyn eagerly picked up the narrative, 'the woman stopped doing her dead man's float, quickly waded the short distance to the jetty, released Rachel's body and floated it out into the pond, then quickly scrambled out under the cover of the weeping willow trees.'

'And by the time the drama with Min was over, and everyone turned back to the pond . . . it was really Rachel Norman's body floating there. And the two killers could just slip away free and clear,' Lucy O'Connor concluded, looking with some admiration at the cook. 'Wow, that was really clever! And even more clever of you to figure it out, Miss Starling,' she felt compelled to add.

But Jenny merely shook her head and smiled fleetingly. 'Oh, I should have cottoned on to it much sooner, really. After all, I saw both the boots and the corset. Both of those should have been enough to worry me and point to the truth, if only I hadn't been so dim and slow off the mark,' she said, sounding disgusted with herself.

'Corset?' Franklyn said.

'Boots?' Lucy said at the same time.

Jenny nodded and sighed. 'I *did* tell you about it,' she said, 'but none of us really gave it the thought we should have. When "Rachel"' — and here Jenny made air quotes — 'went into the pond and almost slipped, her long skirt rode up and I saw that she was wearing modern high-heeled boots. At the time I just thought it was a bit of a gaffe and not very authentic to be wearing modern footwear.' Jenny shook her head over her own stupidity. 'What I really should have been wondering is why the heels were so high, and yet "Rachel" still looked to be the same height!'

'The woman was shorter than her!' Lucy crowed. 'By a few inches?'

'Right — two at least. Maybe even three,' Jenny confirmed. 'And the day before, I'd previously noticed a tight-lacing corset that had been left here on this window seat,' Jenny patted the padded seat beside her, 'and mistakenly supposed that it belonged to Min. I thought she was worried by Rachel's flirting with her husband, and was going to wear the corset to make her lovely rounded figure look thinner.'

'But it belonged to the woman who was going to impersonate Rachel,' Lucy put in. 'I take it our victim was slender? It was hard to tell under all that wet costume.'

'Yes,' Jenny said. 'Rachel was thinner than the woman who helped to kill her, certainly.'

'So. Let's recap,' Franklyn said. 'We know we're dealing with a pair of killers, presumably a tight-knit couple, if they're prepared to kill together. That's one hell of a risk to take, so you have to be sure of your partner. And we know that the female half of the pair is slightly smaller and slightly plumper than Rachel Norman was. We know it wasn't Min and Silas. Ion Dryfuss, as far as we know, came alone and has no significant other — although that will need to be thoroughly checked. But Dr Gilchrist was seen talking to an angry woman, who I now know was his ex-wife, but that could all be a bluff. They might be pretending to be on the skids, but in reality could have been working closely together.'

'Sir?' Lucy said blankly. Jenny too, looked at him thoughtfully.

It took the older man a moment to realise where the confusion lay, and then he waved a hand apologetically in the air. 'Oh, sorry, I haven't told you yet what our Oxford don had to say for himself, have I?' Franklyn apologised to both women. 'According to Rory Gilchrist, he and his wife divorced last year. Vince Braine acted for Rory in the matter. But apparently, the former Mrs Gilchrist started kicking up rough, claiming that Rory had hidden his assets from her during the divorce, and she was determined to hound him into giving her more alimony. And she was getting so persistent that she was starting to make his life intolerable in Oxford, which is partly why he booked this weekend — to get away for some peace and quiet, and also because he wanted to consult again with his solicitor.'

Jenny nodded. 'Yes, that makes sense. I got the feeling from one or two things I overheard between them that Vince Braine wasn't altogether convinced that Dr Gilchrist had been totally honest with him.'

Franklyn smiled. 'I wouldn't be surprised either. When I talked to him, he definitely looked a bit shifty when he had to mention the assets his ex was convinced he'd hidden away.'

'Sounds like they hate each other's guts, sir,' Lucy said. 'I can't see how they'd come together again and trust one another enough to collude in a murder. And why would they? They had no reason to want Rachel Norman dead. Did they?' she asked, turning once more to Jenny for clarification.

'Oh no,' Jenny agreed at once. 'It wasn't the Gilchrists who killed Rachel.'

'So that only leaves us with one other couple who could fit the bill,' Franklyn said heavily. 'By a process of elimination, it has to be Matthew Greenslade and his ex-fiancée. If she really is his ex, that is,' he grunted sceptically.

'We know Rachel came between them,' Lucy agreed. 'And as a member of the am-dram society, Matthew would have access to the inn and the changing room and would know all about Rachel's schedule . . . But don't they both have alibis?' she added, frowning.

'Only those provided by family members,' Franklyn put in quickly. 'And you know how much they can be worth,' he added scornfully.

'But why would they want to kill her?' It was Jenny who asked the question, and for a second it lay flatly in the sudden silence.

'Because she broke them up,' Lucy said, then frowned. 'Except . . . no. Because if I had a fellah and he had an affair with another woman, I might want to kill *him*,' she grinned wolfishly, 'but I wouldn't help *him* kill *her*. Why would I? It doesn't make sense.'

'No, it doesn't, does it?' Jenny mused. 'And why would Matthew want her dead anyway? OK, so she wrecked his engagement,' she conceded, 'but if every man who went astray ended up killing "the other woman," despite maybe having feelings for her, well . . .' She shrugged graphically.

'Unless he was a nutter,' Franklyn muttered darkly. 'I've known men who turn possessive and bitter and jealous and end up striking out.'

'Yes, but this was a carefully thought out crime,' Jenny said. 'It took planning and timing. It wasn't a murder committed in the heat of the moment and in passion or rage.'

'And besides, it took two of them,' Lucy said. 'And Felicity Thornton had nothing to gain by helping him kill Rachel. Unless she was a nutter too.'

Franklyn sighed and agreed that the likelihood of two nutters getting together to carefully plan and pull off a killing, for which they had no real motive, was unlikely.

'Well in that case, who the hell *did* kill her?' he asked, and he was sure he could feel his frustration making his blood pressure rise. 'And why?'

'Oh, the why, I think, is fairly clear,' Jenny said. Then paused and modified that somewhat. 'At least, in general it is. Inspector, I recommend that you get a warrant or subpoena or whatever it is you need, and search the firm where Rachel Norman worked and see if you can track down which lorry drivers working there have a criminal record. I think you'll find that at least one of them must have done time. And if you ask around, I think you'll find that Rachel will have had him wrapped around her little finger. That won't be hard to find out,' she predicted. 'Office gossip and intrigue will ensure that everyone will know who you're talking about. And when you find him and question him, I think you'll also discover that Rachel had found something that he'd told her very interesting indeed.'

Franklyn slowly leaned back in his chair. 'OK, now that sounds rather convoluted,' he complained. 'And don't hint! If you know something, just spit it out.'

Jenny Starling looked slightly hurt at this. 'But I *don't know* anything specific,' she shot back. 'How could I? I've never set foot in Rachel Norman's place of work! I only know from what I've *surmised* that there must be evidence to be found there. And that's your job,' she added.

Franklyn took a deep, calming breath. Beside him, he saw Lucy O'Connor suppress a grin. 'OK. One step at a time,' he forced himself to say patiently. 'You said the reason Rachel Norman had to die was fairly obvious. So, what was it?'

'Well, the one thing that always struck me about Rachel — and you've probably got the same impression from all the witnesses you've been questioning who knew her — was how ambitious she was, and how much she liked money.'

Lucy nodded. 'That's a fair comment,' she said, giving her boss a wary look. 'You've maybe not had time to check out the reports, sir, but everyone we've spoken to from the am-dram people down to her friends have said that Rachel really wanted to make it big. As an actress I mean.'

'Right,' Jenny said. 'Even from the short time I knew her, I heard Rachel say that she was having expensive photographs taken of her by an up-and-coming photographer with a reputation, in order to boost her portfolio and help her get television parts. I heard she's also been having expensive acting lessons too, maybe even paying for a private coach. Anything, in fact, to help her climb the ladder and get parts. And that can't have been cheap.'

'And she was always well-dressed,' Lucy put in. 'I remember reading somewhere one of her friends saying that Rachel liked her bling.'

'She did,' Jenny put in. 'Expensive watch, jewellery, designer clothes. For a girl who worked as a secretary at a haulage company, she dressed like someone from one of those reality shows about rich people living in Chelsea or Belgravia or whatever.'

'But how could she afford that?' Franklyn demanded. 'Her parents aren't wealthy. Of course, she might have had a sugar daddy.'

'We haven't found signs of him so far if she had, sir,' Lucy warned him. 'I've seen the collated reports from the PC's interviews, and if she had an older, richer man in tow, I think someone would have known about it.'

'Oh, almost certainly, I'd have said,' Jenny put in. 'From what I knew of her, she wouldn't have been too shy to boast about having hooked herself a rich lover.' The cook shook her head with a brief smile. 'She wasn't the most tactful of women. She had no scruples in dropping Ion Dryfuss rather brutally, and she couldn't have cared less about Matthew's broken engagement. And she made no bones about making a play for Silas Buckey when she learned he'd recently sold his company and had money to burn. No,' Jenny shook her head again, 'if she was getting her money from a rich suitor, it wouldn't even have crossed her mind to be discreet about it.'

'So where was she getting the money for all this high living and expensive, career-boosting extras?' Lucy said.

Jenny glanced across at Franklyn, one eyebrow arched, and the inspector whistled through his teeth. Slowly, he began to nod his head.

'The good old standby,' he said, making Lucy, who wasn't following this, flush resentfully as the Junoesque cook also smiled conspiratorially at her boss.

'Exactly,' Jenny said succinctly.

'What?' Lucy demanded.

'Blackmail,' Franklyn said flatly.

Jenny sighed. 'Well, as we've said, Rachel was the sort of woman who liked to indulge herself — the best clothes, make-up, what have you. And she had very little empathy for anyone else — and if that isn't the psychological profile of a blackmailer, I don't know what is. And then there were all those arch little throwaway lines she used to give off. Once or twice, when the am-dram people were here and she was giving a performance, afterwards in the crowd, she'd be talking to someone about something apparently innocuous, but all the time I'd get the feeling that she was actually talking to someone else. Or rather, directing her *message* to someone else. And that "little chat" she had with Vince, when she asked him about a person's duty to inform the authorities if they knew of any illegal activity, was a prime case in point.'

'Yes, I picked up on that too,' Franklyn said, not wanting the cook to think that he hadn't.

'So someone around her, someone in the group this weekend, had done something bad, and she knew all about it — probably from some felon she'd met at work,' Lucy said, picking up the baton. 'And she'd been blackmailing that person for some time?'

'Right,' Jenny said. 'She'd been spending money on making sure that her star was rising for quite some time. At least a year, if not longer.'

'So why mention it in public at all?' Lucy said, then quickly held up a hand. 'Sorry, that's obvious. She was piling on the pressure, wasn't she?'

'Exactly,' Jenny said. 'I think her blackmail victims were getting restless. Perhaps they were beginning to cut up rough — threatening to stop making the payments. And they needed a timely reminder of what would happen if they did.'

'So who was it,' Franklyn said flatly. He'd had enough of all the background information, and wanted to get down to the nitty gritty. 'Who killed her?'

Jenny sighed sadly. 'Well, who had access to the inn, and the changing rooms? Who was in a position to kill her and plan the whole charade we witnessed? Who do we know who are a solid couple, working together for the same goals, and feeling sure enough of each other to kill?'

'I don't know,' it was Lucy who said it, the frustration clear in her voice. 'We seem to have eliminated everyone!'

Jenny shook her head. 'Who owns the inn?' she asked quietly. 'Who always seems to be grubbing for money, as if it was a vital commodity? Who arranged the Regency Extravaganza and booked the am-dram players? Who has a business reliant on them being "morally above reproach?"'

'The *Sparkeys*?' Franklyn said, looking over at the empty bar automatically. 'But . . .' In truth, he hadn't considered the landlords of the inn. They hadn't even been on his radar. 'Run it by me,' he said heavily.

Jenny sighed. 'Like I said, I think if you check Rachel's place of work you'll find a driver who did some time in prison, and that he knew Muriel in her younger days. And I also think you'll find, when you check, that she had a bit of a wild childhood. I noticed that she has some sort of a tattoo on her arm — and not the pretty little butterfly kind, but a large, maybe ugly or violent image. I think Muriel must have grown up far from this lovely place, and in rather under-privileged circumstances. At some point she fell in with a bad lot. In short — I think you'll find that she has a criminal record.'

'Which will blow her deal on this place if the trustees of that old lady get to hear about it,' Franklyn caught on at once.

'Right. Think about it. The Sparkeys have worked hard for years to own this place — it's their dream. But then along comes Rachel, and demands payment to keep silent. And then bleeds them dry until they finally snap and come up with the plan to kill her.'

'So they come up with the plan and arrange the Regency weekend, and once Rachel has changed into her costume for her final performance, one of them kills her,' Lucy said.

'I think that must have been Richard,' her boss put in. 'It makes sense — he's the stronger of the two.'

'Yes, I think so too,' Jenny put in firmly. 'Yesterday afternoon, whilst we were waiting about after lunch, I saw Richard leave the bar for a while, then come back a little while later. I think now that he'd just gone upstairs and killed the poor girl. Then he took over the bar from his wife, and Muriel went upstairs to do her part, and change into a costume identical to Rachel's. Don't forget, they'd have had a few days to either rent one or make it up, assuming they'd seen the dress shortly after Rachel first arrived at the inn. They must've found some excuse to see it, or had gone into the dressing room to take a closer look. And they'd have known it would be the black gown, given her final scene.'

'And whilst his wife dressed as Rachel did her bit, he . . . what?' Lucy mused.

'Gathered up his peasant costume with the comical floppy hat that almost hid his face,' Jenny said, 'took his spider in a matchbox with him, put Rachel's body in his car and drove to the back of the pond. And all the time he was doing this, his wife was stretching out her performance to give him as much time as possible. It did seem to take us longer to get to the pond than it really should have done.'

Jenny shrugged. 'And then . . . well, we know how it all played out. Richard would have left some dry clothes and "civvies" behind the weeping willows for Muriel to change into after she got out of the pond,' Jenny said, 'and all the pair then had to do was come back to the inn and prepare to hear the sad news.'

For a second the two police officers were quiet. 'Well, it all hangs together. And makes sense,' Franklyn said. 'But can we prove it?'

Jenny shrugged. 'Surely forensics will find something in his car? And Old Walter may be able to help you confirm what the Sparkeys' movements were that day, if you ask him. After the procession left for the village pond, the inn was left unattended. And Old Walter would have been hanging about as usual, hoping for free drinks. Then the divers will find the recording device, but whether or not it will have survived its dunking, I don't know. But if they can recover Rachel's voice from it, that'll help.'

'And we might be able to find Muriel's costume. Even if she's dumped it or burnt it by now, at least we know what we're looking for,' Lucy said optimistically.

Jenny looked out of the window and sighed heavily. 'And to think, all they wanted was to own a piece of this,' she said sadly. 'To be the hosts of this lovely old inn and live their dream. It wasn't much to ask, really, was it? Just as all Rachel wanted was to live her own dream, and become a star.'

For a moment, there was a heavy silence. 'The things we do in pursuit of dreams, eh?' Franklyn finally said morosely.

Jenny Starling nodded. 'I'm so glad that all I want to do is cook. And that there are plenty of people willing to let me do it,' she said simply.

* * *

The next couple of hours passed in a frantic haze of activity for the two police officers. Warrants were obtained, searches were made, as were arrests. The Sparkeys were taken away, Muriel tearful and protesting their innocence, Richard white-faced and shocked into silence.

Min and Silas Buckey departed for their next destination of Stratford-upon-Avon, looking rather pale and unusually quiet. Ion set off for Wales without a word to anyone. Dr Gilchrist was at the police station making out his statement before departing for Oxford, and Jenny Starling, with the inn closed, had taken the time to clear up in the kitchen, conscientiously putting the perishables away in the fridge and the leftover food in the freezer.

She had just finished packing and was hauling her case downstairs when Franklyn pushed through the door.

'Oh. Are you off?'

'Yes. But you have my home address and contact details if you need to speak to me again,' Jenny said, walking over to the bar and hoisting herself onto a stool. She looked decid-edly glum.

'Cheer up! Why are you looking so down?' Franklyn tried to jolly her along. 'The Sparkeys have already cracked by the way. And you were quite right — the dead girl's growing demands were driving them mad. And they'd finally realised that they'd never be free of her. They were getting desperate, and were convinced they were going to lose everything — their home, their livelihood and their dream. They say they had to kill her — it was almost self-defence.'

But Jenny wasn't even thinking of the Sparkeys.

'It's not that,' she said miserably. 'I'm just wondering how I can tell my friend Patsy that she might not have a job to come back to! With her employers in clink and the inn closed, I didn't exactly do a stellar job of holding her post for her, did I?' she wailed.

THE END

THE JOFFE BOOKS STORY

We began in 2014 when Jasper agreed to publish his mum's much-rejected romance novel and it became a bestseller.

Since then we've grown into the largest independent publisher in the UK. We're extremely proud to publish some of the very best writers in the world, including Joy Ellis, Faith Martin, Caro Ramsay, Helen Forrester, Simon Brett and Robert Goddard. Everyone at Joffe Books loves reading and we never forget that it all begins with the magic of an author telling a story.

We are proud to publish talented first-time authors, as well as established writers whose books we love introducing to a new generation of readers.

We won Trade Publisher of the Year at the Independent Publishing Awards in 2023. We have been shortlisted for Independent Publisher of the Year at the British Book Awards for the last four years, and were shortlisted for the Diversity and Inclusivity Award at the 2022 Independent Publishing Awards. In 2023 we were shortlisted for Publisher of the Year at the RNA Industry Awards.

We built this company with your help, and we love to hear from you, so please email us about absolutely anything bookish at feedback@joffebooks.com

If you want to receive free books every Friday and hear about all our new releases, join our mailing list: www.joffebooks.com/contact

And when you tell your friends about us, just remember: it's pronounced Joffe as in coffee or toffee!

ALSO BY FAITH MARTIN

DI HILLARY GREENE SERIES
Book 1: MURDER ON THE OXFORD CANAL
Book 2: MURDER AT THE UNIVERSITY
Book 3: MURDER OF THE BRIDE
Book 4: MURDER IN THE VILLAGE
Book 5: MURDER IN THE FAMILY
Book 6: MURDER AT HOME
Book 7: MURDER IN THE MEADOW
Book 8: MURDER IN THE MANSION
Book 9: MURDER IN THE GARDEN
Book 10: MURDER BY FIRE
Book 11: MURDER AT WORK
Book 12: MURDER NEVER RETIRES
Book 13: MURDER OF A LOVER
Book 14: MURDER NEVER MISSES
Book 15: MURDER AT MIDNIGHT
Book 16: MURDER IN MIND
Book 17: HILLARY'S FINAL CASE
Book 18: HILLARY'S BACK
Book 19: MURDER NOW AND THEN
Book 20: MURDER IN THE PARISH

MONICA NOBLE MYSTERIES
Book 1: THE VICARAGE MURDER
Book 2: THE FLOWER SHOW MURDER
Book 3: THE MANOR HOUSE MURDER

TRAVELLING COOK MYSTERIES
Book 1: THE BIRTHDAY MYSTERY
Book 2: THE WINTER MYSTERY
Book 3: THE RIVERBOAT MYSTERY
Book 4: THE CASTLE MYSTERY
Book 5: THE OXFORD MYSTERY
Book 6: THE TEATIME MYSTERY
Book 7: THE COUNTRY INN MYSTERY

Made in the USA
Middletown, DE
14 June 2024

55764513R00117